Wilson's
Tales of the Borders

Revival Edition Volume 5

ISBN 978-1-9998312-5-7

Published by the Wilson's Tales Project, 2018.

Design by Jon Goodyer

Edited by Nick Jones, Joe Lang & Fordyce Maxwell

Illustrated by Sheila Vickers

Printed in Berwick-upon-Tweed by Martins the Printers Limited
www.martins-the-printers.com

Contents

The Birth of the Tales:

Success comes at a fatal cost

Andrew Ayre continues the story of Wilson and his Tales: Wilson achieves success at last – but his triumph is all too brief.

In Volume 4, we left Wilson contemplating his future with some anxiety. Despite his success in improving the Berwick Advertiser and boosting its circulation, in early 1834 his position as editor looked to be under threat. The owner's son was coming back from university – and from his correspondence, Wilson clearly felt his job might be handed to the young man.

Perhaps this was the spur Wilson needed to be bolder in publishing his creative work. Despite enjoying some small success with plays and poetry, he had spent much fruitless time and effort trying to persuade other agents to publish his work. Occasionally, he had published his own short tales in the Berwick Advertiser, perhaps as space-fillers when news was scarce. More regularly he had published his poems under the heading of Rhymes by the Editor. These had been well received.

He had toyed with the idea of rescuing a troubled local publication, such as The Border Magazine at Kelso, and making it his own. The main barrier was probably his lack of financial resources.

Instead, he saw an opportunity to start a personal enterprise as a sideline while retaining the security of his salary at the Berwick Advertiser – at least for as long as that might last.

Scottish poet and author Allan Cunningham had enjoyed some success with his Traditional tales of the English and Scottish peasantry – originally written for magazine publication and subsequently republished in book form in 1822. They were said to be 'highly esteemed' by Sir Walter Scott. And following Scott's death in 1832, perhaps Wilson felt there was now a gap in the market…

Writing to his friend Everett on 21 October 1834, he announced he was "about to oppose Chambers journals in some measure or in other words to publish my Tales of the Borders in cheap weekly numbers". William Chambers had begun publishing Chambers's Edinburgh Journal on 4 February 1832 as a weekly broadsheet covering a wide range of subjects. Wilson intended to publish his weekly in a more convenient size, close to what we would recognise as A4.

W&R Chambers continued publishing the Journal until 1956. The firm became a well-known publisher of periodicals and books – including the first edition of Chambers's Encyclopaedia, serialised in weekly editions in the 1860s.

Weekly serialisation was a popular method of publishing in the 19th century, adopted by Dickens and Scott among others. At the end of a series, full editions would be either bound up from individual instalments or reprinted as a single volume – much like a DVD box set at the end of a TV drama series today. Schooling had become more widely available by the early 1800s and literacy levels were rising. Reading around the fire on a Sunday evening had become a popular occupation.

The Berwick Advertiser of 18 October 1834 announced that Wilson's Tales of the Borders would be available from 8 November, priced at three halfpence. They were promoted as being good 'moral tales', to ensure their reading would be permitted in households with strict principles about acceptable activity on the Sabbath.

The first edition was duly published in November 1834 with the help of G. Richardson of Berwick. It contained three tales: The Vacant Chair, Tibby Fowler and My Black Coat; or, The Breaking of the Bride's China.

The Vacant Chair had been published previously, and was in many ways typical of the Tales that were to come. A farmhouse that straddles the border. A son who goes missing. And his story of being kidnapped then pressganged to sea, seeing service and adventures abroad, and eventually returning home many years later to reclaim his teenage love and astonish his parents, who had failed to recognize him.

The second issue started with a tale appropriately called We'll Have Another.

Wilson printed 2,000 copies of the first issue – thought by some to be an ambitiously high number. But before the week was out a second print run was needed to meet unexpected demand. Within a few issues, 4,000 a week were being printed. By Issue 9 on 3 January 1835, the printers were churning out 5,000 a week yet still unable to meet demand. By March the print run had risen to 8,000 and four editions were announced – including one for the south of England, published in London by Houlston & Sons, who were also appointed selling agents.

In Issue 17, Wilson declared that schools were now using copies of the Tales as 'readers'.

And in May 1835, he gave readers of Issue 26 a progress report: "It is now half-a-year since the Tales of the Borders commenced, and their success may excuse the author in saying a few words concerning them. There was never an instance of what is called a provincial publication meeting such a reception from the public: and it is only one or two metropolitan publications that can boast of the same circulation, and that only within the last two perhaps three years. The Tales of the Borders were commenced at about 2,000 weekly. Many said that quantity would never sell. [But] of the earlier numbers more than 17,000 have been sold; and from proposals that have been made to the author by London Book-sellers, to circulate work throughout England, Scotland and Ireland, within a month the weekly circulation will not be below THIRTY THOUSAND."

WILSON'S
TALES OF THE BORDERS.

On SATURDAY next will be published, Number I.,
PRICE THREE HALFPENCE,
OF
HISTORICAL, TRADITIONARY, AND IMAGINATIVE
TALES OF THE BORDERS,
By JOHN MACKAY WILSON,
Author of "The Enthusiast," &c.

THE TALES OF THE BORDERS will be published in WEEKLY NUMBERS, at Three Halfpence each. A Number, containing *sixteen large and closely printed columns*, will be issued every Saturday Morning. The Numbers will be of the same size as the PENNY MAGAZINE, but will contain a greater quantity of matter.

For the convenience of those residing in remote districts, where it might be difficult to obtain the Weekly Numbers regularly, the Tales will also be issued in MONTHLY PARTS at Sixpence, each Part containing *sixty-four columns*, being nearly equal to the matter in an ordinary volume. The work will extend to ninety-six Numbers, or twenty-four Parts, forming two large volumes.

Independent of nearly THIRTY OTHER TALES, the first *five* parts or first *twenty* Numbers, will contain a Novel entitled CLOUDS AND SUNSHINE, which in itself would occupy THREE VOLUMES of the same size with those of similar works sold at £1 12s 6d. The reader of the Tales of the Borders will therefore have the same quantity of matter for *Sixpence*, as in such publications would cost the purchaser *Twelve Shillings*.

OPINIONS OF THE PRESS.

"As a Tale writer J. M. W. bears away the bell from all the writers in the Annuals."—*Spectator*. "In the straightforward character of his genius, he is worth them all."—*Sun*. "His feelings are warm and his sympathies powerful, and he paints with a pathetic hand the emotions of the heart."—*Athenæum*. "One of a trio of Wilsons who are an honour to their native land."—*Paisley Advertiser*. "One of whom Scotland has cause to be proud."—*Albion, of New York, May 3d, 1834.*

Orders and Subscribers' Names received by all Booksellers, and by the Agents appointed for the sale of the Work, a list of whom will be advertised.

A discount of threepence a shilling will be allowed to Agents and others taking more than fifty copies, and where less than fifty are ordered of twopence.— Settlements monthly, with an additional discount of two and a half per cent. where payment is made within a week from the date of the monthly account.

Published by JOHN MACKAY WILSON, Tweedmouth, Berwick-on-Tweed, to whom, or to the Advertiser Office, all orders should be addressed; and it is particularly requested that orders for the first Number be forwarded on or before Saturday November 1st.

A publishing phenomenon of its time! With his tales of ordinary people caught up in events historic or imaginary, Wilson had caught the public's imagination: they could perhaps readily identify with many of the characters, circumstances and hardships experienced.

Wilson had finally found the success he had craved – but at a price. As well as writing the Tales and dealing with their printers and distributors, he still had to keep up his day job as editor of the Berwick Advertiser. His health deteriorated. What seemed at first to be a mild illness in the autumn proved fatal. He was just 31, and less than a year into his project.

Wilson's death was announced to his readers in early October 1835, in Issue 49:

"It is our painful duty to send around the land the tidings of the lamented death of Mr John Mackay Wilson, the author of these Tales…

The event we thus deplore, took place on the morning of the 2nd instant. Thirty-one short years only had rolled over him in this vale of tears. His sun had not yet gained its meridian splendour, when the dark cloud of death overshadowed him, and has left us to look after him in sadness across that bourn no traveller ever returns."

The exact cause of death is not clear, but contemporary sources talk of him having over-exerted and over-stimulated himself in his efforts to keep everything going. One imagines a mix of physical exhaustion and perhaps an opiate habit – as alluring to creatives then as now – to keep up his efforts.

Wilson's obituary told readers:

"He has left a widow respectable and respected; and, from what we have said of his struggles through many a dark year, she is left to depend on the profits of his works for the comforts necessary for her, till she sink to rest with him in the grave."

Readers are reassured that 'tales yet untold' are held in reserve: publishing is to continue and they are implored to continue subscribing to support his widow.

Wilson had originally intended to publish 96 issues. He died as the 49th was published. But the Tales continued – becoming a much larger and more enduring venture than even Wilson could have dreamed of. More of how that happened in Volume 6…

The Wife Or The Wuddy

"There was a criminal in a cart
Agoing to be hanged —
Reprieve to him was granted;
The crowd and cart did stand,
To see if he would marry a wife,
Or, otherwise, choose to die!
'Oh, why should I torment my life?'
The victim did reply;
'The bargain's bad in every part —
But a wife's the worst! — drive on the cart.'"

In the 16th and 17th centuries night time raids over the English and Scottish borderlands and the river Tweed were rife. Night raiders, or reivers, consisted of both Scottish and English families. Nationality mattered not, questions of property or land ownership were dealt with by force and stealth, regardless. Might was right; resorting to the law "unmanly". One of the boldest exponents of this lifestyle was William Scott, Lord and heir of Harden, of Oakwood Tower on the River Ettrick. His family motto "We'll have moonlight again." was one the young Lord was ever keen to give effect to.

This tale begins one October night when young Scott called his men to arms.

"Look friends, is it not a sin and a crying shame to see things going so awry? Manhood is all but extinct in the Borders. A bit scratch with a pen upon parchment is more effective than a stroke with the sword. A child now stands as good a chance to hold and have, as an armed man with a hand to take and to defend. Such a state of things benefits those who are too lazy to ride by night, and too cowardly to fight. Never shall it be said that I, William Scott of Harden, was one of their number, conforming to such a state of affairs. Give me the good, old, manly law, that 'they shall keep who can,' and with my honest sword will I maintain my right against every enemy". Tonight, this strategy was going to be engaged against the Scotts' oldest foe, Sir Gideon Murray of Elibank, a man whose insults and slights would no longer be ignored.

"So", he continued "what say you, neighbours, will you ride with me to Elibank so that, before morning, every man of them shall have an empty byre?"

A score of men set off, stout and bold, mounted upon light and active horses, and armed with muskets and staffs, each with a good sword.

Arriving at Elibank before dawn, not a single Murray was seen abroad. Unchallenged they set about emptying the byres. Collecting together horned cattle and sheep, they drew them into an immense herd, intending to drive them through the forest to Oakwood. Scott of Harden was the rearguard.

As he rode, he exalted that whilst "There will be dry breakfasts in Elibank at Oakwood that night an entire bullock shall be roasted, and all shall eat of it."

Simon Scott, a family servant of forty years and relation to the Lords' family, challenged this plan. His strongly held view was that to roast a whole bullock would be a terrible wanton waste and an overindulgence of the estate dependents, moreover it was bound to foster discontent.

"Well argued, good Simon," Harden replied; "but your economy is ill-timed. After a night's work such as this there is surely some licence for celebrating. I say it - and who dare contradict me?"

But the servant did dare and the debate continued until it was interrupted by the deep-mouthed baying of a sleuth-hound; followed by a loud cry, as if from fifty voices, of "Tonight for Sir Gideon and the house of Elibank!"

Sir Gideon was a knight whose name struck a note of terror in the heart of his enemies. As a foe he was fierce, resolute, unforgiving. Never known to turn his back upon an enemy, nor forgive an injury. He understood justice in its severest sense, but not compassion. A stranger to mercy, he regarded the life of any man who had injured him no more than a worm to tread underfoot. Middle-aged now, none of his three adult daughters were considered fair, and all were very unmarried.

Being an experienced reiver he remained one step ahead of his enemies. Harden had not, as he believed, come upon him as "a thief in the night". Whilst Harden prepared for the foray, Sir Gideon's spies alerted him to it. That not a Murray was astir upon their arrival was an illusion. Eyes were everywhere, including those of the Old Knight and his fifty followers.

"Quiet!" he growled. Then, speaking in a deep and earnest whisper, he continued. "Patience, men! You shall have work before long."

As Harden and his followers began to disperse in the depths of the forest, driving the cattle, they heard Sir Gideon hail, "Now for the onset!"

"We are followed! Halt! To arms!" cried Harden.

A few men were left in charge of the scattered herd, whilst the rest spurred back their horses as rapidly as the forest allowed. They arrived speedily, but too late, such had been the stealth of Sir Gideon that young Scott and Old Simon could only cry out in surprise when Murray bellowed "Willie Scott! Yield quietly, or a thief's death you shall die, right here."

"While a Scott of Harden has a finger to wag, no power on earth shall make his tongue say 'I am conquered!' Even if the odds were ten to one I should not turn my back." replied Harden, defiantly.

"I intended to grant you small mercy, but not after those words. Men, humble these Hardens." continued the Knight.

"Arm! every Scott to arms!" replied Harden. "Sir Gideon, if you insist on raising arms your only legacy will be your "fine featured" daughters, unwed and unwanted, for all of your men, including any who in pity might offer one their hand will be dead."

"Harden, you shall rue your words. Insult me but not my children."

The fight began. The strife was bloody and desperate. Men grasped each other by the throat, holding their swords to each other's breasts, set to introduce their enemies to eternity. The reports of muskets, the clash of swords and clang of shields played against the neighing of maddened horses and lowing of frightened cattle. The howl of the sleuth-hounds and shouts of angry men mingled wildly together. There followed the low melancholy groans of the dying. Harden's scattered troops were slain, wounded, or overpowered. He had his sword broken in his grasp and his horse struck dead beneath him. Surrounded, he and old Simon were captured by the Murrays, at which his men fled, abandoning their spoils.

Thus Sir Gideon recovered all that had been taken from him, as well as capturing Harden and Simon, rich prizes. Returning to Elibank, Lady Murray welcomed and congratulated her husband. Her mood altered on seeing the heir of Harden a captive. Mindful of the little mercy her husband was likely to show, as a mother she reflected on how she would feel if he was her child. Thrust into a cell the prisoners were told that the following day they would be hung upon a tree.

The last revelation shocked Simon. The prospect of being hung like a dog, rather than shot or beheaded, a disgrace. Failing to account for the birth and rank of his master and unbefitting of their status as gentlemen. And he said as much to his Master.

Ordering him to silence, Harden continued. "Let Murray hang us in his bedchamber. The manner of death matters little, how we meet it is what counts. Any shame rests with him."

Simon gained no solace from the reply, fretting for his family. Not afraid to die, he simply did not welcome such an unnatural and ignominious end. Harden, trying further to placate and quieten him assured Simon that his family would be provided for by the Oakwood estate.

Meanwhile Lady Murray addressed her husband inquiring of his intention for the young Lord. The Knight directed her gaze to an elm tree. "To-morrow, my dear, young Harden and his kinsman shall swing there together, or I am no Murray."

"I think that you are acting cruelly and foolishly." said his wife.

"I care nothing about the cruelty, what mercy did any Scott show to me or to mine? And what do you mean by saying I act foolishly?"

"Only this," You have three daughters who need marrying and there is a dearth of suitors. It isn't every day that you have a potential husband for one of them in your hand."

"Wife, for once you are right" he replied, "there is more wisdom in that remark than I would give you credit for".

So it was decided. The following day Harden would be given a choice. Either, marry their eldest daughter Agnes, locally known as Meikle Mouthed Meg, or hang. His wife was confident Harden would choose marriage. The Knight less so, saying "I would rather die a death that was before me, than marry a wife I had never seen. But prepare Meg for becoming a bride, I shall see what the intended groom has to say."

Obeying her husband she went to Meg, quickly turning the conversation to her daughter's age and the question of marriage, and extolling what good fortune it would be if Meg secured a good man. Meg acknowledged this but noted there was a greater likelihood of "the Ettrick River running through Yarrow" than of it happening, given her appearance. Undaunted her mother asked Meg what she thought of young Scott. Meg, shocked at her mother speaking so when the lad was to be hung, said "if I could save him I would." Her mother, satisfied at this reply, told Meg that if, come the morning, Scott petitioned for her hand, and she accepted, then there would be no hanging.

Meg, is unpersuaded, doubting that even if she were to beg on bended knee her resolute father would change his mind.

Meanwhile, Sir Gideon goes to Harden and makes the offer.

"Now, ye rank marauder, I will give you a chance. You shall choose between a wife and the wuddy tomorrow."

He explained that the wife would be his daughter Meg; and the wuddy, the nearest tree, where he would hang until his fleshless bones dropped.

Simon enquires if the Knight intends a similar fate for him, offering, if ever he became a widower, to marry the girl himself.

Young Harden, angered, orders Simon to keep his cowardly thoughts to himself, and turns to Sir Gideon, defiant.

"I appreciate such mercy. Not only will you spare my life but you are willing to give me "bonny" Meg in marriage. The truth is that there is no love lost between us. Even if the offer included all of your lands I would still not accept it. If our current roles were reversed I would not hesitate to hang you. So do your worst, there will be Scotts enough left to revenge my death."

Sir Gideon, furious at this rejection, determines he shall die the next day and let those who dare avenge the death. Simon petitions his Master. Why should he too be sacrificed, breaking the hearts of his family, because of his master's stubborn refusal. Then, reminding him of the sanctity of life and how unnecessary death should be avoided, he finishes by promising to marry any of Sir Gideon's daughters if ever he becomes a widower.

"Audacious idiot!" the Knight responded to this last, striking Simon to the ground.

Harden, riled, berates the Knight for baseness in attacking a fettered prisoner, asking "where is the Murrays' pride now?"

Sir Gideon, feeling the truth of this rebuke, withdrew, simply reminding Harden that at twelve the next day he must choose a wife or the wuddy.

Harden remains defiant. "The gallows be it, my choice is made. Trouble me not again."

Simon suggests that it is a woman's temperament, not her looks that matters. Harden calls him a fool and a coward and again bids him be quiet.

Close to midnight a woman dressed as a domestic enters their cell.

"What or who do you want?" inquires Harden.

"To speak with the lord Harden, and to ask if he has any dying commands that a poor lassie could fulfill for him."

"Dying commands!" Simon doesn't miss the chance; "Oh, those are awful words, yet my Lord remains foolhardy, refusing marriage?"

"Who sent you, maiden, and who are ye?" continues Harden.

"Lady Murray's servant girl, sir, in whom ye have a true and steadfast friend; though I doubt that, having refused Meg, her intercession can help now."

"Why has Lady Murray sent you?"

"She is a mother, with a mother's heart; and, as you have a mother and sisters who will mourn for you, she thought that you might wish to send them a final message. I offered to be your messenger."

"Maiden!" came the emotional reply. "Do not speak so for you will unman me, denying me the right to die as becomes my father's son."

"That's right girl" whispers Simon; "speak to him about his mother, then we may get him to marry Meg, and I shall see my family again."

"What are you whispering, Simon?" snaps his Master.

"Oh, nothing," came the innocent reply. "I simply asked that if you sent her over to Oakwood with a message, she inquire for my poor widow, Janet, and my children and tell them nothing distracted me in the hour o' death but thoughts of being parted from them."

Disregarding this reply, Harden, addressing their visitor, says "You speak as a kind and considerate lassie. I will send a note to my poor mother."

"And, no doubt you would like to hear any answer, or to learn how she bore the news of your fate?"

"So I would, but alas by the time you return I will only feel my mother's sorrows with the sympathy of a disembodied spirit." replies Harden.

The maid is confident that, if he wishes to await a reply, she can, through Lady Murray, secure a reprieve. Harden is not keen. To him accepting any clemency is a sign of weakness. He wants his mother to be clear, she must seek to avenge his death.

Simon, seeing the advantage of delay, urges the girl to seek a remission. Harden, keen to be left to meet his fate, asks the girl to seek a reprieve for his servant only. Simon says that all he wants is for his master to meet Sir Gideon's daughter, before choosing death over her. If, however, his Masters' choice is death, he will die with him.

"And have you decided on the wuddy without even seeing poor Meg?" asks the maid.

"I have not seen nor heard her, but I gather she is so plain that no man would wish to have her shadow him through his life's journey," the laird replies.

"Truthfully, she has been misrepresented. Seeing her you might change your view. Anyway, if all that can be said against her is that she is not so bonny, is that so bad?"

"Silence, lassie! I will not be forced. I have no wish to see her face. You, though, speak with a feeling heart, and so I trust to you my last letter to my mother. But first, let me be assured my confidence is well placed. Let me see your face."

Throwing back her cowl, she spoke. "You will see as little in my features as you expect to find in my mistress Meg's. But remember, jewels are often encrusted in coarser metals, and many a delicious kernel is to be found within an unsightly shell."

"Ye speak sweetly, and sensibly so," he said, looking at her. "Although your are plain, there is honesty and kindliness written upon every feature of your face. I trust you. Have you a pen?"

"I have one with me. Your letter shall be faithfully delivered." And she vows to see him spared until he receives a reply, and to do all she can to secure his freedom.

Handing the letter to her, Harden felt a tear trickle down his cheek. Simon asks that she visit his family, and tell his wife that, should she ever remarry, he would haunt her day and night!

Early next morning Meg speaks with her father. "Father, I understand that it is your pleasure that I shall this day become the wife of young Scott of Harden. Is it not due to the daughter of a Murray of Elibank to be courted before giving her hand. The young man has never seen me and knows nothing of me. Never will I disgrace you by giving my hand to a man who only accepted it to save his neck. Of course, if you command it I will marry him, but it is a big step, and I would like to get to know him first. Could you give a weeks' grace for this to happen?"

"Meg," replied her father. "I never thought you had the gumption to say what you have just said. But your request is useless, for he has already, point blank, refused to marry you. The only outcome to this refusal is that he be hung, today."

"Don't say that father! I beg you, allow me four days to know him. If after that he doesn't make a request to marry me without a dowry, then I must look even worse than is said of me!"

"All right, four days, Meg, for your sake. However, if Harden still refuses, he and his half-crazed companion shall hang." Assured, Meg left, pondering how she might save the prisoners and secure a husband.

Meanwhile Harden's mother sat amongst her daughters, waiting for news of her son. The household wept on receiving news that he was Murray's prisoner. The thought of losing her only son overwhelmed her, a torture so great that she promised vengeance upon the Murrays. Then a girl appeared, bearing a message from Harden with a note, and a promise to take back any answer she wished. The girl's presence piqued the woman's curiosity, she wanted to know more of this kind soul who had taken such an interest in her son at this perilous time.

"I am merely a despised lassie," the maid told her, "but one that would risk her own life to save either yours or his."

"Bless you" replied the Lady, as she opened her son's letter. It read:

Dear, honoured mother,

Fate has delivered me into the power of Murray of Elibank, the enemy of our house. He has doomed me to death, and I die to-morrow. Do not sit and mourn me, wringing your hands and tearing your hair. Rouse every Scott upon the Borders to rise up and be my avenger. If you lament the loss of a son, do not spare the Murrays - neither son nor daughter.

Poor Simon o' Yarrow-foot is to be my companion in death. He whines like a lass over his fate, and yearns for his wife and bairns. On that account I forgive him the want of heart and determination. See that his family are provided for.

As for me, I shall meet my doom with disdain for my enemy in my eyes and on my tongue. Even in death he shall feel that I despise him; and a proof of this I have given him already; for he has offered to save my life, providing I would marry his daughter, Big mouthed Meg. A proposal I have scorned!

"Ye were right, Willie! ye were right, lad!" exclaimed his mother. Bursting into tears as she acknowledges how wrong he was and how precious and desirable was life. She wished, that for her sake alone he had married the lassie, whatever she was like. Turning to the messenger she asks "And what is the young lady like, the marrying of whom would save my Willie?"

"Well, she is not generally considered a good catch. But there are many as would make a worse wife. Her looks, though no better than mine are at least not further marred by a glum countenance."

"Well, if you're right, he should marry her. But, he's both stubborn and proud, like his father. You'd have a better chance of moving the Eildon Hills as forcing him to do something he doesn't want to."

Reading the last part of her son's letter, she noted his enthusiasm at the kindness shown him by the fair messenger, and of the promise she had made to liberate him if possible, adding:

And if she does, whatever be her parentage, on the day that I should be free, she should be my wife, though I have preferred death to the hand o' Sir Gideon's comely daughter.

"Lassie," said the lady, weeping, "my boy talks greatly of your kindness. For that my heartfelt thanks. Might I accompany you to Elibank? If you cannot free him, perhaps, if I saw him, his heart would soften and he might agree to the marriage."

On hearing this, Meg, for it was she, offered a final audience for mother and son and a safe return thereafter. And so the two women journeyed together, Lady Scott disguised as a peasant,

Back at Elibank Harden watched the sun rise on his last day. Simon on his knees in prayer. When the watchtower bell tolled noon, Simon again entreated his Master to marry Meg, to avoid their unnecessary deaths. To no avail.

Sir Gideon appeared. Too proud and impatient to spare the men for four days, despite his promise to his daughter, he announced they would hang next day.

That evening the gentle maid once more returns to the prisoners' cell.

Harden, touched again by her kindness, said that he would like to reward her if he could, before enquiring of his mother and how she planned to avenge his death. Simon too asked after his family, only for her to tell him "I trust it may be longer than you expect before she is widowed, or marries again, but that depends on your master."

The maid tells Harden of his mother's heartbreak, explaining that she would rather have another daughter than lose a son, and hopes he will marry. Gobsmacked and defiant, he vows to obey her in anything but this request, wishing only to know how she intends to avenge his execution.

Here the maid intercedes. "I think you are wrong to reject and despise Meg before you have seen her. She may be better than you believe. Some as good as you have said they would marry her if they could. Take my advice; see her and speak with her before you make a rash decision."

His reply was sympathetic but emphatic. He was determined that it would never be said that Gideon Murray had terrified him into marriage to save his life. He was sure mother would agree after her grief subsided.

"Well," replies the maid, "If you won't listen to me, maybe you will listen to another." At this Lady Scott enters the cell falling into her son's arms.

"O my son! Marry Meg and save yourself for all our sakes!"

Harden, blinded by his still stubborn pride, replies coldly "I will never accept life upon such terms," adding "And you shouldn't be here. If Murray finds you he will ransom you for your freedom."

 "The kind messenger brought me, she promised Murray will learn nothing of my visit. Willie, as you love and respect me, do not throw your life away, marry Meg! Her looks matter not, I am told she is kind."

Harden does not waiver in his resolve.

And so at five to midday with the maid Lady Scott must depart, heavyhearted.

Noon beckons, the warder calls "It is the hour! Prepare to die!"

An angry Sir Gideon returns. "Well, youngster. The hour is come. What is your choice?"

"Lead me to execution. I know that with the hemp around my neck, in contempt to you and yours, I will spit upon the ground where you tread."

"Guards, lead forth the said William Scott of Harden to execution. Hang him upon the nearest tree, and let him remain there until the boldest Scott dare to cut him down."

Turning to Simon Murray tells him he is free, warning such mercy will not be extended if they catch him again.

"No!" says the honourable Simon. "My Master shall not die alone."

"So be it", acknowledges Murray.

The two prisoners are led towards a tall elm. Sir Gideon's wife, daughters and retainers are all present to witness their execution. As the hangman prepares, Meg approaches her father, a veil over her face. Sinking on one knee, she begs a simple favour.

"You certainly pick your moments Meg! Go on then, what is it?" he asks.

As she whispers to him his countenance exhibits a variety of expressions, from indignation to surprise. Ordering her ""Rise up, Meg" he approaches young Harden. "For your sake he shall have another chance to live."

Then, to Harden, "You have chosen death over my daughter's hand. Would you marry the lass who has been helping you and your mother rather than die?"

"If anyone else asked me, I would say yes, giving my heart and lands too, but, for the sake of the Scott clan's pride and honour, I..."

He never finished the sentence, for, at that moment, his mother ran forward, saying, "But another does indeed ask. Me, Lady Scott, your very own mother."

Then Meg, raising her veil, stepped forward, saying, "And I, Meikle Mouthed Meg, over whom you choose the wuddy, also requests it."

Shocked but delighted, Harden clasps Meg's hand, acknowledging her efforts to save him, a proud young man who has treated her with nothing but disdain. And she asks him directly, "So, do ye prefer the wuddy still?"

Which is how a day that began with preparations for execution ended in a joyful marriage. Knighthood was conferred upon Young Harden. He and Meg had many children, and she was said to be one of the best wives in Scotland. Whilst Simon declared that he never saw a better-looking woman in Ettrick Forest, his own wife and daughters not excepted.

Retold by Denise Bradshaw

The Wife or the Wuddy Companion Piece

The late 13th to the early 17th centuries were the years of the Border Reivers. The long wars between Scotland and England had created "the debatable lands" where the rule of law and royal authority was intermittent and weak. Families on both sides of the border raided livestock and goods from anyone within riding distance regardless of nationality. The only bonds were those of kinship. To this day the term "freend" (friend) is used to denote family as in " he's some freen o' oors" meaning he is a relative of ours. The names of the reiving families on both sides of the border still fill the telephone directories. So Elliot, Armstrong, Scott, Graham, Johnstone, Jardine, Lindsay, Kerr, Turnbull, Crozier, Douglas and Rutherford are from the South of Scotland; whilst Charlton, Dodds, Milburn, Heron, Ridley, Collingwood, Stokoe, are from the North of England. There are many others.

When raiding, or riding, as it was termed, the reivers rode on hardy nags or ponies renowned for the ability to pick their way over the boggy moss lands. They wore light armour or jacks (a type of sleeveless doublet into which small plates of steel were stitched), and metal helmets hence their nickname of the "steel bonnets". They were armed with lances and small shields, and sometimes also with light crossbows known as "latches", or later on in their history, with one or more pistols. They invariably carried swords and dirks. The distances covered on raids show how tough were these men and their horses. Night time was the choice for ride-outs.

Will Scott, the hero of this Wilson's Tale had as his family motto "Reparabit cornua Phoebe" which was interpreted by his countrymen as "We'll hae moonlight again," meaning "we'll keep on raiding our neighbours."

Blood feuds were common and long-standing and alliances short lived though sometimes made more permanent through marriage. It was a time of lawless men and grieving women; of daring deeds and savage reprisal; of plunder and banditry; of occasional chivalry and courtly manners.

The tales of these exploits, the skirmishes, raids, rescues, duels, fights as well as the loves and liaisons were told from pele tower to bastle house by the minstrels wandering through the country, welcomed at any hearth. Their songs, and it is now sometimes forgotten that they were songs, were part of an oral tradition, memorised and repeated over centuries. Sir Walter Scott committed them to paper in his Minstrelsy of the Scottish Border, thus probably saving them for posterity with their stark economy of word and evocative phrases,

"...the Lindsays flew like fire about,"

"...the child may rue that is unborn, the hunting of that day!"

The mother of James Hogg, the author, was the source of much of Scott's material and as she said, "There war never ane o' my sangs prentit till ye prentit them yoursel an ye hae spoilt them awthegither. They were made for singing an' no for reading; but ye hae broken the charm now an' they'll never be sung mair".

It is interesting that, despite the violent patriarchal nature of this society with its emphasis on exploits of arms and manly courage, many of the ballads tell their tale from the female point of view, from that of the widow, mother or unwed girl. They also show that the women of the reiving times were no mere chattels or ciphers but strong minded, astute defenders of their families, firm supporters of their rough-riding spouses and lovers.

The story of the mistress of the house serving spurs on an empty platter to signal that the larder stores were low and something had to be done about it, is common to family lore in several clans on both sides of the border and is particularly associated with the wife of Walter Scott of Harden. It may also have been that the wandering harpers and bards, knowing full well who was in charge of the hospitality upon which they relied would, while recounting the feats of the menfolk, skilfully create a female interest in their stories. It would be those same women who would sing the songs to their children down through the generations to the time of Hogg's mother.

In addition to his own prodigious literary output and his collecting of the ballads, Sir Walter Scott was assiduous in his researches into the ancestry of the many branches of the Scott clan. It is from him that we get the story of "Muckle Mou'd Meg".

This was adapted by Alexander Leighton when he took over the researching and publishing of Wilson's Tales after John Wilson's untimely demise in 1835. He renamed it "The Wife or the Wuddy." This title was also adopted for a volume of poems and songs by Canadian poet Wellington Brichan (1812-1885). It runs to some 1,400 rhyming couplets!

There are a number of possible interpretations for the word "wuddy". It seems it is a corruption or local pronunciation of widdy which is in itself a Scottish version of withy, referring to a band or hoop of twisted willow used as a halter and thus, by association, a noose for the gallows. Wattie Wudspurs, grandson of Auld Wat, was so-called because, in this case, Wud seems to mean mad or headstrong, which fits the character.

The Scotts of Harden were descended from Walter Scott of Sinton, whose second son, William Scott, was the first laird of Harden. He acquired the estate from Lord Home in 1501. William Scott was called 'Willy with the Boltfoot,' from a lameness caused by a wound which he received in battle. Despite this, he was an expert horseman and spearman.

Situated with good defences, high above a deep ravine, Harden House is nearly four miles west of Hawick. The present House of Harden dates from the 17th century. It succeeded an earlier tower which was destroyed about 1590. One of the most famous of the Scotts of Harden was "Auld Wat", one Walter Scott (1550?–1629?).

In June 1592 he assisted Francis Stewart, Earl of Bothwell, in his attack upon Falkland Palace and, with his brother William and other Scotts, helped Bothwell in the winter of 1592–3 to plunder the lands of Drummelzier and Dreva on Tweedside when they carried off four thousand sheep, two hundred cattle, forty horses, and goods to the value of two thousand pounds. He also, with five hundred men, Scotts and Armstrongs, joined Sir Walter, first Lord Scott of Buccleuch, in his famous rescue of William Armstrong of Kinmont, 'Kinmont Willie,' from Carlisle Castle in 1596. A feat triumphantly recounted in the ballad of the same name.

This Walter Scott married, about 21 March 1576, to Mary Scott of Dryhope, called "The Flower of Yarrow", of whom the story of the spurs on the plate is told. They had five daughters and four sons. The eldest, William Scott, succeeded to Harden and seems to have inherited his father's free-booting spirit. He resided in several of the fortified houses owned by the family but favoured Aikwood (Oakwood) Tower situated on the banks of the Ettrick.

The Scotts and the Murrays were ancient enemies; and, as their lands were adjoining at many points, they had many opportunities of exercising their enmity "according to the custom of the Marches." Scott of Buccleuch had supported King James IV in his abortive attempt to oust one John Murray - The Outlaw Murray - from his lands in the Ettrick Forest. In the event the monarch had to yield to Murray's power and appoint him Sheriff of the Forest. The ballad "The Sang of the Outlaw Murray" gives a vivid account of the encounter between king and subject.

By the time of Muckle Mou'd Meg, the Scotts had acquired much of the lands held by the Murrays in the past. Nevertheless, the lure of raiding the old enemy was too much to resist. The handsome, dashing young laird led an expedition over the Yarrow valley and the Minch Moor to Elibank on the Tweed, the home of Sir Gideon Murray. Unfortunately for the dare-devil, Scott of Harden's reivers were caught in the act of driving off the cattle and their leader captured.

Elibank Castle

Sir Gideon was all for hanging Harden the next day and had him imprisoned in Elibank Castle to await his fate.

It is at this point of the Tale that the practical reasoning of the lady of the keep, Lady Margaret, dampens the impetuous rage of her husband when she reminds him that he has three daughters, all described as "ill-favoured" and not likely to be easily married off. Agnes, nicknamed Muckle Mou'd Meg is the eldest. Murray considers the proposal and makes the offer to his prisoner of marriage or hanging. It is recounted that, at first, the young man preferred to be hung! He later recants and is married.

It is recorded that Agnes and William Scott had a long and successful union resulting in five sons and three daughters. Their third son, Walter or 'Watty Wudspurs' features in the ballad Jamie Telfer of Dodhead when he recovers the stolen cattle of the afore-mentioned Jamie with a few extra for good measure! Obviously the daring blood of grandfather Wat and father William ran in his veins.

In the Tale of Muckle Mou'd Meg, Wilson expands the story giving a greater role to Meg and the other women and creates a foil for the defiant Harden in the almost comic remonstrations of Simon the retainer.

The accuracy of Sir Walter Scott's account has been questioned as there exists two copies of a marriage contract between the two showing that the marriage of young Harden and Agnes Murray, instead of being a hurried business, was arranged very leisurely, and with great care, calmness, and deliberation by all the parties interested, including the two principals, the bridegroom and bride, and the parents on either side.

Instead of one contract, as is usual in such cases, there were two separate and successive contracts, made at an interval of several months, before the marriage was finally arranged. The first contract is dated and signed in Edinburgh on18th February 1611. In it, William Harden and Agnes Murray agree to solemnise their marriage in church, within two months after the date of the contract. Stipulations are made in the document for the investment, by Walter Scott, of his son and his promised spouse, and their male heirs, in the lands of Harden and other lands belonging to Walter and William Scott; and Sir Gideon Murray, on his part, becomes bound to pay to William Scott the sum of seven thousand merks as tocher (dowry) for his daughter. The contract is subscribed by Sir Gideon Murray, William Scott, and 'Agnes Murray,' all good signatures. But as Auld Wat of Harden could not write, his subscription is thus given: 'Walter Scott of Harden, with my hand at the pen, led be the notaries underwritten at my command, becus I can not wryt.'

Od! hear our gudewife, she wad fain save your life;
Wat Scott, will ye marry or hang?

It may be that the couple were hand-fasted at their first encounter as was the custom at the time. Once this binding declaration had been made there would have been time for the formalisation of the union to be done with due legality at a later date. The second contact may have been due to Sir William trying to wriggle out of his enforced nuptials but, having paid a dowry, neither Gideon Murray nor, indeed, Wat of Harden was going to let him do so.

There must have been a good basis for the story as William Scott died in 1655 and his famed descendant, the writer Sir Walter Scott, was born in 1771, so the story had been around for a hundred and fifty years by the time it was committed to paper.

James Hogg, the Ettrick Shepherd, custodian of much of the border lore and oral tradition, recounted the affair in his poem The Fray of Elibank. He supplied such detail about the various allies and kin of the Scotts who took part in the raid that it has the ring of authenticity.

The story of William's dilemma, a choice between marriage to an "ill-favoured" woman and death, is recognised with wry humour and universal appeal. It has been recounted and celebrated in poetry, prose, theatre, music and art.

In 1856 James Ballantine produced a fair homage to the border ballad form in his poem, though he gets the names wrong, appearing to confuse William with his father Walter.

Robert Browning in his rooms at Balliol College, produced an anglicised version after reading the story in Scott's Tales of a Grandfather.

Muckle Mou'd Meg has now been immortalised in sculpture at Elibank, between Innerleithen and Galashiels.

Aikwood Tower, the erstwhile home of William and Agnes, is a few miles to the south. It was restored by Sir David and Lady Judy Steel is now available as a wedding venue.

How appropriate!

Background by M.A.FENTY

The Royal Bridal

Lamberton Moor was a colourful sight for several days in the summer of 1503, as thousands gathered for the arrival of young Princess Margaret of England and her marriage to King James IV of Scotland.

This arranged marriage to bond the nations drew all classes together on the Scottish side of the low, but symbolic, border dyke. Knights, nobility and their followers postured among the tents and flags. Plays written for the occasion were performed. Morris dancers capered. In the public area, crowds drank as they watched athletes wrestle, jump, put the stone and throw the hammer.

What was uncertain was whether James, a young man known to most of his subjects only by reputation as a generous and courageous playboy, was in the magnificent Scottish royal pavilion. If he were, how many would, or could, recognise him?

While speculation continued, so did the games. The star was Robin Meikle. Over six feet tall, broad-shouldered with powerful arms and legs, Robin dominated the putting and throwing and could beat all-comers at wrestling and cudgels.

Or almost all.

Among the hundreds watching was a man famous locally as Strong Andrew: a lean, tough fisherman from Eyemouth who had beaten Robin in contests several times and was keen to do so again.

Andrew was a bachelor. So he had to be his own cadger and sell the fish he caught, having no woman to do it for him. But sales were good at Lamberton, and only fear of leaving his takings unguarded among a light-fingered crowd stopped him tackling the increasingly cocky Robin.

At last, ambition overcame caution. Andrew was about to take the ring – when a young man of middle size, dressed as a nobleman's servant, beat him to it. As Robin confidently tried to make a traditional 'Hawick hug' hold, the young man, almost casually and without removing his hat, took him off balance behind the knee and threw him.

The spectators roared, Andrew among them. As he mounted his pony to head home, he congratulated the stranger: "Well done! I'm as glad as though I'd been given a gold coin!"

Fish sold well again next day. Andrew was cheerful as he started for Eyemouth, overtaking on his way the stranger who had thrown Robin. "Losh man," said Andrew, "is it you? I've done nothing but think of you since yesterday when I saw you take the brag out of that big bullock."

Andrew had a second motive for conversation. He wanted to wrestle; but he was uncertain whether the stranger – as a nobleman's man – might imitate nobility and, as he put it, "treat a cadger body as though he were different flesh and blood".

The stranger laughed and quoted an old saying: "Why, the King may come in the cadger's way!"

True, said Andrew, and a king might find the cadger more like himself than he thought. "Now, sir," he went on, "will you let me try you in a friendly way?"

"Certainly, friend," said the stranger. They gripped and Andrew, beaten as easily by the stranger's technique as Robin, was flattened. As he got up he said: "Sorrow take me if I thought there was a man in 10 parishes could have done the like. But it was a fair fall."

They walked on together to a public house run by a widow, Nancy Hewitt, and her daughter Janet. "I usually stop here for a drink," said Andrew. "If you have no objection, we'll take a stoup together."

Nancy served them, and Andrew asked after Janet in a way that suggested more than friendly interest. The stranger, who had heard of Janet's good looks, sat increasingly silent and thoughtful.

"This is no time to be sad," said Andrew, "when the King is merry, the country merry, and we should be cheerful together." As a man of 33, he snapped his fingers at unhappiness. And so should a young man like the stranger. "So let's drink the health of bonny Jenny Hewitt!"

"With all my heart!" said the stranger, and they drank before Andrew burst into cheerful song. As the song ended, Jenny came in. The stranger turned his attention to her immediately with a flurry of flowery compliments. The shy young woman was embarrassed, but pleased, by flattery that felt like a dagger to Andrew's heart.

Rip that smooth tongue out of his head, he thought: I'll let her see if he who has the glibbest tongue has the manliest arm.

But before he could act, the stranger broke off his stream of compliments to ask for food. All Nancy had were haddocks that Andrew had left with her that morning. Good, but small, she said: two would not be enough so she "would gut three".

"Certainly gut three," said Andrew. "I brought the stranger in, and what is a haddie and what are they worth?"

"You're a generous-hearted fellow," said the stranger, "and I'll call you Gut-three if we meet again."

After eating, another drink. But as it was poured, Andrew's pony broke loose and he raced after it. When he returned minutes later, he found Jenny struggling in the stranger's arms and Nancy shouting: "Scoundrel!"

Andrew hit hard and the stranger went down. Clambering up bleeding at the mouth and preparing to fight, he said: "You'll be sorry for that."

Before they could fight, Jenny cried out and Nancy pleaded for the good name of her house. "Andrew!" she said. "I thought you had more sense."

"Sense!" said Andrew. "If it had been the King himself laying a hand on my Janet I would have served him the same."

"You brag largely and freely, neighbour," said the stranger, throwing a gold coin on the table. "But we'll meet again with no women to interfere." The money, he said, would buy "bonny Janet" a gown and bodice.

"Take your money," said Andrew. "I brought you in and I'm paying."

"Don't be daft," said Nancy, tucking the coin into her pocket. It wasn't every day, or week, or year, that she saw a gold coin. Andrew and the stranger could only scowl at each other and part.

Three days later, Princess Margaret arrived.

The sun glittered on the sea, on Lindisfarne and Bamburgh castle to the south, St Abb's Head to the north, the Cheviots to the west, on Halidon Hill and on the purple heather of the moor. Thousands gathered from the east of Scotland to join the Scottish nobility as the English procession approached – heralded by cannon roar from Berwick, led by the Earl of Surrey and the Earl of Northumberland, and followed by thousands of Northumbrians.

All eyes would be on the royal couple and James, though reluctant to marry even for the sake of his country, put on a good show. He rode to meet his bride in black velvet, fine satin, crimson edging, precious stones and gold spurs.

Dismounting, he entered Lamberton Kirk, where Margaret waited with her advisers and protectors. Seeing that reports of her beauty were true, he responded immediately by dropping to one knee and kissing her hand. After the brief official marriage ceremony they walked to the royal pavilion to watch knights from both nations take part in a tournament.

The knightly action was courtly, but too stiff and formal for an impatient King James. He left the dais with excuses to his new wife, muttering: "I must put spirit into this".

Within minutes, the Savage Knight appeared, face hidden by a visor, his body in a skin-tight suit, a javelin in one hand, a spear in the other. In short order he fought and beat three of the tournament knights to roars from the crowd. There was no fourth challenge and the Savage Knight walked round the ring to take the applause.

As he passed where Andrew and Janet stood, his visor slipped and Andrew exclaimed: "Confound me, if it isn't the very chiel I clouted on the lug in your mother's! Credit for what he's done, but he's no more a knight than I am!"

While he pondered that, the main event of the day was about to take place: a no-quarter battle between Borderers and Highlanders, with rewards for all who showed courage and a gold purse from the king for the bravest of all.

Andrew began to twitch, tense his muscles and move towards the ring. Here was his chance to make his fortune and marry tomorrow. Janet tried to stop him, arguing they had enough to live on without risking his life.

She failed. As the herald asked for one more Borderer to complete the team, Andrew stepped forward, borrowing a knight's sword to take part in what proved to be a deadly and savage fight. Men went down injured or dying, several to Andrew as Highlander after Highlander fell to his sword. He was the champion of the field, the hero of the fight.

The King, urged by a young Queen horrified by the butchery, signalled an end to slaughter as the home crowd roared "Eyemouth yet!" and "Wha's like Andrew!"

Janet at last dared to look – and saw Andrew come towards her. But before he got there he was summoned to the King for his reward. Unnerved by the prospect, no matter how brave he had been in battle, Andrew approached the dais under escort and head down.

"Look up, brave cock o' the Borders!" said King James, smiling. "Goodness, man, you must have an ugly face if you need to hide it after showing such a heart and arm."

Andrew raised his head and the king recoiled: "Ha! Traitor!"

Recognising the stranger he had wrestled and punched, Andrew exclaimed: "I'm a done man!"

"Seize him!" said the king.

But Andrew was gone like a startled deer, sword in hand as the crowd parted, before disappearing into the sea-banks. The King's men were told to search until they found him and bring him bound before the King.

As the search began, the King prepared to leave – changing into a cloth of gold edged with sable. Riding a horse adorned with jewels, with his bride seated behind and followed by a hundred peers and nobles, he left for Edinburgh.

Many in the big crowd cheered. But others were silent, puzzled by the King's treatment of a hero, and said: "It bangs all! We're sure Andrew never saw the King before. He was never 10 miles out of Eyemouth in his life. The King must be mistaken – and Andrew was foolish to run for it."

Janet, stupefied and terrified, struggled to her mother's home and wept. She couldn't bring herself to explain, but witnesses from Lamberton were soon passing through with the tale, keen to talk about what had happened and to embroider it with claims that the King had demanded Andrew brought before him "dead or alive".

About midnight the frightened women heard a gentle knock at the window and a familiar voice whispering: "Janet! Janet! It's me."

Once he was inside, Nancy said: "Andrew, what have you done? What is really the meaning of it?"

"You might well ask," said Andrew. "But who do you think is the King? Now, just think."

Nancy was baffled: "Who can the King be, but just the King?"

"Ah," said Andrew. "You remember the chiel that came here with me the other night, that left the gold for the three haddies, and that I gave a clout in the chops for his behaviour? Yon was the King."

"Yon the King!" cried Janet.

"Yon the King!" cried her mother. "Have I really had the King of Scotland in my house, sitting at my fireside, and I cooked a supper for him? Ah, he's a bonny man!"

That was not what Andrew or Janet wanted to hear. Janet said: "Mother! Bonny here, bonny there! He's threatening Andrew's life. What shall we do?"

As she wrung her hands Andrew said: "That's just the thing, hinny. I have to get to the other side of the Tweed before morning and I'm only here to say goodbye. If I can't get back to marry you, will you come to England?"

Of course, she said. But before that she would go to Edinburgh to plead with the King for Andrew's life. If he refused to listen she would threaten to tell his young Queen of what he had said and done to her.

They talked too long. A dozen armed men pushed into the room and seized and bound Andrew. As they hustled him away, Janet shouted: "But the Queen shall know everything!"

Within two days Janet and Nancy had joined Andrew as prisoners in Edinburgh, accused of trying to hide a traitor. On his fourth day in captivity Andrew was hauled before a frowning King James, seated in a large room in the castle and surrounded by armed men with naked swords. Andrew bowed. He expected to die, but showed he was unafraid.

The King said: "Now, traitor. Do you deny that you raised your hand against our royal person?"

Andrew, undaunted, replied: "No."

"You heard that, kinsmen," said the King. "A confession of guilt from his own lips. What should the punishment be?

"Death," said the nobles. "The traitor's doom."

The King said: "No, we shall be less just than merciful. Because he fought bravely at Lamberton, we will spare his life. But the hand raised against our person shall be cut off. Prepare the block!"

The block was brought. Andrew knelt with his arm laid bare and the executioner stood with sword drawn, waiting for the King's command. But there was an interruption as the young Queen and attendants came into the room.

"What can I do for you, my fair Queen?"

"A favour, my King," she said. "A favour that you don't cut off this audacious man's hand, but that you chain that hand for life.

"Be it so," said the King. Taking the executioner's sword, he touched the kneeling Andrew on the shoulder and said: "Rise up, Sir Andrew Gut-three. And now we chain your offending hand…"

As he spoke, the Queen raised an attendant's veil to reveal Janet. The King took her hand and placed it in Andrew's.

"Am I dreaming?" said the reprieved man. "Oh, Jenny. Oh, Your Majesty. What can I say?"

"Nothing," said King James, "but that the King came in the cadger's way."

Retold by Fordyce Maxwell

The Royal Bridal Companion Piece

The noun 'cadger', a 15th-century northern English and lowland Scottish term for an itinerant scrounger – more generously tinker or peddler – has long since fallen into disuse. But its descendant, codger, remains with us. And the verb is still going strong: we all occasionally cadge a lift.

The Royal Bridal is a fictional tale grafted onto a loose retelling of the marriage between a Stewart king and a Tudor princess. James and Margaret are flesh and blood. Robin Meikle, Strong Andrew, and Janet and Nancy Hewitt are creatures of Wilson's imagination. The encounters between the border folk, who to my mind are the truly honourable characters of the Tale, and their royal betters are fiction. But Wilson's Tale nevertheless captures certain central features of the reign of Scotland's sixth Stewart king, James IV: violence, royal splendour, and the King's promiscuity.

James's reign was forged in war and extinguished in war. The 15-year-old prince was a full rebel participant in the civil war that, in June 1488, saw his father James III murdered as he left the field, defeated, after the Battle of Sauchiehurn. It was regicide, not patricide – though the young James may have seen it differently, for it was said that for the rest of his days he wore a chain belt around his waist in penance. He reigned until that dreadful day, 9 September 1513, when in the mud and rain he led his army down the slopes of Branxton Hill to annihilation at what came to be known as the Battle of Flodden.

The marriage was not a love match. Relations between Scotland and England in the late 15th century were not very much more peaceable than they had been in the preceding two centuries; yet there was a desire for the enmity to come to an end. Peace suited James, whose vision of an independent Scotland engaging actively in European diplomacy with France and Spain was hampered by constant auld enemy struggles. As for Henry VII of England, his most ardent wish was to secure his still-fledgling Tudor dynasty for his progeny, a task that would surely be made easier if the threat of a Scots or possibly even Auld Alliance invasion spilling across his northern border could be obviated. To both men the intertwining of the Tudor rose and the Scottish thistle would be a perfect dynastic, if not romantic, match.

Negotiations in the Scottish border town of Ayton in 1497 resulted in a seven-year peace treaty which on 24 January 1502 metamorphosed into the grandly misnamed Treaty of Perpetual Peace. Its central provision: "Between the Kings of Scotland and England, their heirs and successors, their kingdoms and subjects of every degree that there be a good, real and sincere, true, sound, and firm peace, friendship, league and federation to last all time coming". To seal the deal, in a side agreement entered into the same day, it was contracted that James would marry Henry's daughter, the 12-year-old Margaret. He was 16 years her senior.

Wasting no time, James and Margaret were betrothed the very next day at Richmond Castle. Margaret was present in person. James was represented by his proxy, the Earl of Bothwell, who no doubt was speaking with the utmost sincerity when on behalf of his king he pledged to the bride to "take thee into and for the wife and spouse of my said sovereign lord, James, King of Scotland, and all others for thee forsake". All others, that was, except James's myriad mistresses, who included one named Janet. All would be revealed to Margaret when in the late summer of 1503 she made her first visit to Stirling Castle.

Having attained the age of 13 and therefore being considered to be of child-bearing age, Margaret began her journey northwards to meet her husband and king on 8 July 1503. Travelling through England's north-eastern lands, she was welcomed at York, Durham, Newcastle, Morpeth and Alnwick. Towards the end of the month she arrived at Berwick, the Scottish border town that had fallen into England's heinous hands some 21 years earlier, where the locals treated her to a couple of days of their favourite sports: bear baiting and dog fighting. On 1 August she rode on to the Lamberton kirk Wilson describes in The Royal Bridal.

It is at the kirk where the Tale and the actual events of Margaret's royal progress to meet her husband king cross – though ever so fleetingly, and only to swiftly diverge. The progress was led by the Earls of Surrey and Northumberland, with an English entourage 2,000 strong. They were met at the kirk by the Archbishop of Glasgow, an array of other clerics and nobles, and 1,000 Scottish guests. The bride was received by a fanfare welcome, followed by a reception and chivalric games held within a grand four-sided pavilion, giving her a first glimpse of the royal splendour for which James would become famous as one of Europe's Renaissance princes.

James, however, was not present. Nor was he expected to be, as the royal couple's Edinburgh marriage ceremony was still a week away. Neither was there a murderous no-quarter-given battle between Borderers and Highlanders. It was only in Wilson's mind that Margaret the teenage princess witnessed the slaughter of the Highlands' best at the hands of an Eyemouth cadger. And if there were any Hawick hugs, they were exclusively of the friendly variety.

The welcoming celebrations over, Margaret spent the night at Fast Castle, from where she travelled to Dalkeith before finally arriving in Edinburgh on 7 August for her marriage the following day. James had spared no expense in ensuring his bride would want for nothing. A new palace had been built at Holyrood, though it is not known what Margaret made of James's chambers being on the south side and hers being on the west. And on arriving shortly after the wedding day at Linlithgow Palace, hers as part of her dowry, the new Queen of Scotland stared in wonder at its magnificence.

It was a different story at the newlyweds' next destination, Stirling Castle. It seems it had not occurred to James to give his blushing bride a little forewarning of the fact that the castle housed the royal nursery. Happily at play were James's illegitimate children – at least six of them, by at least four different mothers, one of whom was Janet Kennedy. Here, even in the red mist of her anger, it must surely have dawned on Margaret that fidelity was not a quality she would find in her husband. And so indeed, through their 10-year marriage James retained his mistresses, Janet included, and Margaret accepted with due stoicism that her principal duty was to ensure the continuation of the Stewart line by producing an heir. Eventually, after seeing three children die in early infancy, on 10 April 1512 Margaret duly fulfilled her duty – bearing a child who would on his father's bloody death at Flodden become the little-remembered James V of Scotland.

By 1512, relations between the auld enemies had once again deteriorated. James no longer had a father-in-law, Henry VII having died in 1509, and was instead in dispute with his brother-in-law: the young, hugely ambitious King of England and would-be King of France, Henry VIII. With James making every effort to revive the Auld Alliance, the Treaty of Perpetual Peace was hurtling towards oblivion. War came in 1513. While Henry was trudging aimlessly around France, James gathered his army in preparation for an invasion of north-eastern England. A pious man, if adulterous, James prayed at St Michael's church in Linlithgow for divine support for his forthcoming campaign. What he received instead was a warning from a yellow-haired, blue-gowned apparition. Beware, the unwelcome visitor cautioned, avoid female counsel and let no woman "tuitch thy body nor thow hairs".

In late August, James's army forded the Tweed near Coldstream and took Norham Castle. A few days later, James was so enjoying the company of the lady of the house and her daughter at Ford Castle that he allowed his army to rest. And during this pause the English army, under the command of the Earl of Surrey – the same man who had in 1503 escorted the young Tudor rose into Scotland for her intertwining with the awaiting Scottish thistle – moved north.

When the two armies faced each other at Flodden on 9 September, James had already lost the initiative – and in the midst of the ensuing battle lost his life. His widow later remarried, badly. Meanwhile, Robin Meikle, Strong Andrew, and Janet and Nancy Hewitt waited patiently to be conjured up several centuries later in the wonderfully vivid imagination of J M Wilson.

Background by Keith Ryan

Beans & Bacon

The Tale of Toby Toothpick

Come, Miss Thalia, you and I have been
Confounded strangers for these 10 years past;
In fact your laughing face I've never seen,
But your sad sister, glooming, o'er me cast
A shred of her black mantle – I'm as lean
As though upon the earth I were the last
Of living creatures; with the fields all tinder,
And the vast world one lifeless, sapless cinder.

Now, Ma'am, you know it is a downright bore,
When any moping, melancholy fellow,
Who looks eternally as though he wore
Death written on his forehead, strives to tell a
Tale of deep passion, or attempts to soar
Into fair fancy's regions, while his yellow
And half-closed eyeballs throw a jaundiced blight
O'er all and everything within his sight.

But, Ma'am, I need not tell you for you know it,
And everybody knows it – or they should –
No gloomy fellow ever was a poet.
Give me the men who every ill withstood,
Who, wounded, bleeding, still disdained to show it –
They who are ever in a laughing mood
Where laughter is acceptable – and then,
Though proud as Lucifer, behold the men

By whom the veil of mystery is riven,
Who handle hearts as playthings, and could wing
Their flight from shades of misery to heaven!
Then come, dear Thaly, I intend to sing –
Provided always that your aid be given –
Of Mister Toby Toothpick: once the king
Of jolly wits within a country town,
But now 'hard set', 'done up' and 'broken down'.

Three days had passed, and not a bit of victual
Had Toby tasted, while his teeth were grinding
Between his meeting jaws a watery spittle!
And dreadful was their eager grate on finding
Nothing to gnaw upon! Ah, Miss! 'Twould set all
Creation's teeth on edge, if angst were binding
Each month to two poor pennyworths of bread –
Which (for a month, poor soul!) was all he had

Each week to live on – sometimes scarcely that!
A month had passed since he had left his lodging,
And he was friendless, houseless, knew not what
On earth would now become of him; for judging
From all he hoped, or knew, he might have sat
Down on the earth and died sans farther trudging.
But Toby, who disdained a beggar's name,
Was made of the right stuff – a thorough game;

Who would have braved the Devil, or been driven
As far beneath the earth in want and pain
As ever that black fellow was from heaven,
Ere he would beg or scurvily complain.

Nay though his eyes were sunk, and his heart riven,
And death before him danced, he would disdain
To shed a tear; for the poor slave is no man,
Who would whine o'er his sufferings like a woman.

Poor Toby wore a coat that once was black,
Upon his feet a slipper, and a shoe.
At hide and seek the winds played through his back –
I mean through tattered coat and spare ribs too:
And then his unexpressibles! Good lack!
They, with his stocking heels, said "How d'ye do?"
To the unfeeling elements, from a score
Of mouths that witness to his colour bore.

It was not far from Cambridge – Toby sat
Vainly endeavouring with a crooked pin
To tack the broken brim upon his hat
By the wayside; half thinking 'twas a sin
For gouty knaves who could not walk with fat,
To live at all, when lo, he looked within
A piece of paper near him, and behold:
Out peeped a heavenly angel – good as gold!

A 20 shilling Bank of England note!
Some may be glad, but Toby was ecstatic;
He leapt with grateful rapture, and forgot
His shoulders and knee joints were still rheumatic –
"Begone dull care" was echoed from his throat,
Though lying-out had made him quite asthmatic,
And as he tripped off, now resolved to dine,
He saw the King of Prussia on a sign.

'Twas on a Saturday, and by the clock
Just five and 20 minutes after seven;
When Toby entering, like a general spoke;
He called for ale, and straight the ale was given;
A crust and cheese – 'twas ate; a pipe to smoke;
He quaffed his ale, and felt at once in heaven.
Within the kitchen, many a country lout
Gazed on his weekly score chalked round about.

The bread and cheese were swallowed in a minute,
And made a hungry man more hungry still;
So Toby's stomach like a starving linnet,
Chirped melancholy music; while to swill
The cold home-brewed which had no substance in it,
But whetted appetite. Resolved to fill
Each craving crevice quite, he bade them spread
For him a table, and prepare a bed.

Now Toby, though his garments were but mean,
Had something of the gentleman about him;
His manners plainly said that he had been
Something before Dame Fortune chose to flout him.
And by the way, the landlady had seen
The Bank's sure passport, and his change had brought him;
Which, when the others saw, and he looked darkly,
They whispered: "Zounds! I'll bet it's Captain Barclay!"

"Sir, supper's ready," said the smiling dame,
And she was round and ruddy, plump and fat,
Clean, tidy, rather bustling, as became
Her age and occupation. Toby's hat
Was in his hurry left – for he thought shame
To keep it on his fine head while he sat;
She took it up; but lo! The crooked pin
From her soft hand tore half an inch of skin;

And on the floor down fell the brimless crown.
Toby blushed black as night at the disaster,
Ashamed the wretched article to own,
While loud mine hostess bawled for sticking-plaster.
He, sweating with vexation, stooping down,
Took up his hat, and walked a little faster
Towards the supper room than he intended –
But beans and bacon this misfortune mended.

And to a hungry man, a glorious sight
The King of Prussia parlour did afford;
In fact, the very essence of delight,
And epicurean glory crowned the board;

A goodly glass of brandy sparkly bright,
A pint of ale, much more we might record,
But last not least, adorning his tweens,
Appeared the bacon and the smoking beans.

By threes, by fours, the beans go one and all,
Slice after slice, the bacon disappears;
"Hunger to him," cried Toby, "who would fall
On 20 shillings and to spend them fears –
Aye, and enjoy them! Now I think I shall
Try the old lady's Glo'ster." And the tears
Dropped down his cheeks in consummate enjoyment,
His whole soul rapt in sublime employment

Of satiating hunger! Of the cheese
He ate till he was satisfied, and then
The ale he drank, and held his sides at ease;
(His vest had long been buttonless) and when
He had sipped-off the brandy – "If you please
You may remove the cloth and fill again
This glass, and bring the papers," Toby cried,
But nothing save bare plates mine hostess spied.

Cheese, beans and bacon, save a crust of bread
There was no solitary fragment left,
All, all were vanished, or devoured, or fled!
Wondering where she stood, awhile of speech bereft,
Stared most expressively, then shook her head;
Thinking no doubt, it was a kind of theft
To pay for supper when she set it down,
And then devour the whole for half-a-crown;

Ale, brandy, all inclusive. Toby said,
She looked when she beheld that all was done
Like one whose reason for a time had strayed,
Stammered as she had neither lost nor won
Most pitifully stupid; but it made
No difference to Toby. When the sun
Did him next morning from his slumbers waken
He still was dreaming of his beans and bacon.

While yet he rubbed his eyes and lay at rest,
Blessing the mem'ry of the man unknown –
But yet of architects the first and best –
Who first invented beds to sleep upon,
Yea while half dreaming, feeling almost blest,
He heard mine hostess in a fearful tone
Exclaim – "The note is forged! Well! No! I never! –
He's yet in bed, transport the wretch forever!"

"Forged!" shouted Toby, springing from his bed,
He seized his trousers, high the window threw,
Leaped to the ground and all but naked fled!
But Toby's flight was vain, for ere he two
Short miles had run, he back again was led;
And bade to hope and liberty adieu.
In vain he vowed his innocence; and he
Fourteen long years was sent beyond the sea.

There still of beans and bacon did he dream –
And every slice became a bristled boar,
While from his heart he fancied blood to stream,
As with their tusks his heaving breast they tore.
But there at length did Fortune on him beam,
Nor long the convict's hated garb he wore,
Wealthy he grew – and as his wealth increased,
Each year he held a beans and bacon feast!

Wilson had always been a poet and promoted himself as something of an expert on the subject, a view shared by other contemporary comment of the time. He lived at a time when literature or "prose" was starting to be become respectable as an art form. Poetry having been seen as art and prose as rather common or vulgar. Indeed Walter Scott was so worried about the possible damage to his reputation that his early novels were published anonymously or under a pseudonym, Jedediah Cleishbotham being one of the more imaginative ones.

As well as publishing his own poetry where he could, before his return to Berwick , Wilson had been a rooming lecturer in poetry. In the days before television there was often an audience to be found in regional towns for knowledgeable speakers. The Manchester Times reports of on one such lecture at the Mechanics Institution over 3 evenings of the 12-14th April 1831.

He is described as an elegant and absorbing public orator. "The lecturer is not engaged in his work, before he ... convinces every listener both of his skill and of his power." "In his recitals, his sudden transitions from the pathetic to the stern, the tragic to the comic, the rapid to the slow, the soft to the loud, - accompanied by every variety of action, look and expression of feeling, can only be equalled by some of our best dramatic performers".

He is also considered to be knowledgeable on his subject, complimented by his own writing skill. "He has the art of at once seizing that which gives prominence and character to the poetry and the genius of the writer, and of striking off the whole in two or three bold sentences, illustrating the same with some daring and often beautiful imagery..."

The report also tells us that though a manuscript lies before the lecturer, composed of leaves apparently of all sizes, they are apparently only referred to occasionally and act as "a reserve rather than a spring from whence he is taking in constant supplies".

Once he had settled in Berwick, we would no longer have the opportunity to give these lectures, but the notes would no doubt form the backbone of his essay on poetry that opens his publication "The Enthusiast".

This was published from Berwick by him in 1834 and opened with his essay on poetry. It then contained his rather long poem called "the Enthusiast" about love a love affair in a setting that sounds a lot like the banks of the Tweed near Berwick , leaving one wondering if there is an element of personal input as he had a teenage dalliance with girl from Gainslaw Hill some 4 miles or so upstream from Berwick. The poem was set out in 2 Canto's and ran to some 40 pages. The poem would also be republished in "The tales of the Borders", but under the name of "Edmund and Helen; A metrical tale", which in latter editions under Leightons editorship, became part of "The Minstrels Tales".

The initial chapter of the book is Wilson's essay on poetry, which he explains: "There are few subjects so little understood and unduly appreciated as poetry". However he is also quick to comment that one needs to be careful what one considers to be poetry. "I believe that out of every hundred verses that are written. Ninety-nine will be found guiltless of possessing even the shadow of poetry."

He next describes the attributes of a "true poet", who amongst other attributes "he must grapple as with the power of an archangel, and play with the feebleness of a worm. He must grasp a mountain, and peep into a molehill."

On poetry's place in the scheme of life he comments "History is the mere body of events – poetry is their soul".

There then follows a rather odd section when he suggest Napoleon's military manoeuvres are poetry in motion. Though he takes care to end the section praising Scots heroism in case anyone should think him too much of a Francophile!

We then get a run through the poets of note starting with Chaucer, as England produced no poets of note before him. This covers Shakespeare to Milton, with special mention to Scots' poets, though he notes no two write with the same dialect or use of language. He gives particular praise for Berwickshire's poets, including Thomas Lermont of Earlston , more commonly known as "Thomas the Rhymer" and Drummond of Hawthorndean who "first introduced sweetness and elegance".

He sums up by stating the opinion that poets are rather special and different people. "Genius is a wild, an unsettled, and a wayward thing" and that as a result, "Poets, like paintings, to be seen to advantage, ought in general to be viewed from a distance"

The book also contained a further 31 poems of varying length and interest. Some were romantic. "A women's love", recites his appreciation of the love of a good women and "The temperate man's song" explains to his drinking companions why he would rather return home to his wife than carry on drinking with them.

> "It's true I like a social gill,
>
> A friendly crack wi' cronies,
>
> But I like my wife better still."

"The Suicide" is somewhat darker as the title suggests. As is, "Thy will be done", subtitled, "written during the prevalence of cholera in Berwick";

> "Death like a silent spirit roams
>
> Around from door to door!
>
> No warning voice proclaims- he comes! –
>
> He glanceth – and 'tis o'er!"

It tries to make sense of the random choice of victims and seeks God to "spare us from thy wrath".

The poem we have chosen to republish in this revival edition is however entitled "Beans & Bacon". A humorous tale of fortune and misfortune and back again. The gist of the story being that a tramp, called Toby Toothpick, picks up a scrap of paper that turns out to be a £20 note when he unfolds it. Making the most of his good luck, he books into the first Inn he finds and orders himself a large plate of beans and bacon, accompanied by a generous quality of ale. He then retires to the comfort of a warm bed to be awoken by a commotion down stairs in the morning. He soon realises the cause for this is that his note has used turned out to be a forgery and he's in trouble. He jumps out the window in his underpants and tries to make good his escape up the road but is soon apprehended. He is taken before the court and the Judge will have none of his excuses and story of how he came across the note in question. He is dually sentenced to transportation to "distant shores". A brutal punishment, but one that was in reality often given by judges sympathetic to the plight of minor "criminals" whose actions where not heinous, but the only other option open to them was often the death sentence.

This however proved the making of the tales hero. It was a chance to reset his life and have a fresh start in a new place without the baggage of his previous precarious existence. In due course he thrived and became a successful and wealthy man of the colonies. In recognition of the event that changed the course of his life, which he still saw as his good fortune, he celebrated the anniversary of the day he found the counterfeit note with a large banquet for all his friends and staff, at which he of course served "Beans & bacon"!

Wilson wrote the preface to The Enthusiast in December 1833 and it was published in 1834 by William Tait of 78 , Princes Street. (Presumably Edinburgh). He wrote of the success of the publication in his correspondence to Everrett, reporting in January 1834 that he was sending 12 copies to him by coach. He also reported having had good feedback from the likes of Lord Howick .

He also wondered whether it would be a financial as well as critical success.

"The copies I have sent out on order on Saturday and today amount to about sixty pounds but it puzzles me to know how I am to get the money collected being from nearly three hundred individuals in different parts of the country, but all respectable"

Very few copies of this publication now seem to exist. The project has so far only come across two copies in existence. One copy is held by the Literary and Philosophical society of Newcastle and is part of their book collection in their rather wonderful library near the Central Station. Well worth a visit. The other copy is held by the Berwick Borough archives. A rather special edition, as it has an inscription gifting the book to his brother James and an ink self-portrait taped onto the inside front cover. This copy was also owned by George Beattie of Amble, one of Wilson's few descendants from his sister Isabella, whose family gifted it to the town.

Wilson also clearly at this stage had plans to start publishing his Tales of the Borders as the family copy also has an advert for their forthcoming publication at the back! Though it is possible this was bound in at a later date…

Background by Andrew Ayre.

The Disasters of Johnny Armstrong

Berwick-upon-Tweed, 24 June 2016. The day after that referendum, Johnny Armstrong heard someone taking the stairs two at a time to his flat. The door was thrown open. His only son, Johnny Junior, a lumpish lad in his twenties, rushed in, panting, red faced, holding a piece of paper up in triumph.

"Dad, Dad, it's..."

"Don't tell me, it's bound to be 'Remain'".

"No, not that Dad...it's you!"

"Yes, Johnny lad, I know I'm me, and, to the best of my knowledge, have been for the past sixty five years, two months and, let me see, six days."

Therefore born 18 April 1951.

"Yes, Dad, I know, but..." Johnny Junior, used to his father's pedantries, could barely contain himself.

Johnny Armstrong, a widower, was a stout, thickset little man with a round, good humoured, ruddy countenance. He had lived all his life in Berwick-upon-Tweed, rarely venturing beyond. Last time was for his cousin's wedding in Brechin. Thirty years ago. He'd never forgotten that attractive girl he'd met...or the stolen kiss at the back of the marquee.

Following in his late father's footsteps, he ran the family ironmongery business in Hide Hill. But out-of-town shopping, and national chains, put paid to that, so he sold up and took early retirement. Father and son still lived in the flat above the shop, now a coffeehouse franchise handy for a flat white, or a frappuccino.

"But what? Why the sudden excitement? Has the Royal Border Bridge collapsed, or have the Russians taken over the Guildhall?"

"No, Dad, nothing like that. It's you! Your number's come up."

"In a good way... I hope." Johnny pinched himself to make sure.

"In a brilliant way, Dad, you've just won a couple of grand on the lottery. Imagine, now we can have a holiday."

"Holiday? Holiday? You know I've never had a holiday, why start now?"

"Because a change is good for you, and you've just won two grand on the lottery."

"Well, I can think of better things to spend it on than a holiday."

"Oh come on Dad, this is a chance in a lifetime."

"Don't rush me. I'll think about it, but, if we do go anywhere, it's on two conditions. One, you come with me, I don't fancy travelling alone. Two, we go somewhere nice."

"So that's a no to Amsterdam then?"

"Three conditions. Nowhere in Holland."

Johnny was a man of fixed views. His Holland-phobia stemmed from when a Dutchman complained about a cast iron skillet. Johnny refused a refund and the skillet flew through the window, knocking off a passing policeman's hat, which led to complications.

"Of course I'll join you. As to where to go, well I think I can guess. That boring place where Aunt Hilary lives."

"How do you know, JJ, you've never been to Brechin."

"I went with Mum and Harriet, remember. You stayed to run the shop. I must have been five."

"Summer 1998. So, five years, two months, and, let me see, three days, assuming you went at the beginning of August."

"I'm sure you're right. Anyway, I hated it. It rained all the time, and I got bored. By the way Dad...the referendum result. It's not 'Remain'... it's 'Leave'."

Johnny, for all his pedantry, wasn't the brightest penny in the pound, and sometimes got the wrong end of the stick. As with this Brexit business. He didn't follow the news much, but he'd voted "Remain", reasoning that he wasn't going anywhere. When JJ told him the result he was surprised so many wanted to "Leave", especially as he'd never heard of this Brexit place that people talked about.

That evening, mulling over a second pint of IPA at the Brown Bear, the penny dropped. Brechin. Of course. They meant Brechin. The only place he wanted to go. But why would everyone else want to go there too? There must be something special going on.

He didn't usually down more than a couple, but tonight he ordered a third to the surprise of Brenda, the barmaid.

"What a day for the country eh, Mr Armstrong! Celebrating, are we? Or drowning, perhaps?"

"Oh, celebrating, undoubtedly."

Despite familiarity with the walk home, Johnny was surprised by a few uncharted obstacles ...a raised paver here, loose cobbles there, a lamppost appearing unexpectedly. He'd made up his mind. They'd go to Brechin next day, not just to find out what the fuss was about, but also...he smiled to himself. He wouldn't tell the cousins, just arrive out of the blue, make it a surprise. Heading down Hide Hill, he nearly bumped into another unforeseen lamppost, lost in wondering if that attractive lassie he'd sat beside at the wedding breakfast was still about. Perhaps this "Leave" idea wasn't such a bad one after all....

Next morning Armstrong father and son were up early to catch the 09.30 to Edinburgh Waverley. Johnny made sure they were at the station in good time. He certainly didn't want to miss their train. Johnny Junior, a keen trainspotter, hoped to see a rare train en route, probably in Craigentinny Yard on the approach to Waverley. He was disappointed that Brechin was no longer on the railway network. It had been closed on 4 August, 1952, when, Johnny calculated, he was just one year, three months and seventeen days old.

Johnny Junior, running ahead of his father saw that the 09.25 Glasgow service was ten minutes late. Then he noticed that the next train south was a special charter. Johnny was coming down the stairs from the footbridge.

"Dad, there's a special due through any minute, I'm going up to the end of the platform to get some photos."

"OK, son, I'll see you on the train. Don't forget, Coach F, seats 24 and 25."

But Johnny Junior was so busy photographing the special, hauled by a rare Class 37 Deltic diesel in original BR livery, that he missed his own train. He could see his father waving frantically from Coach F, Seat 25 as it pulled away. More interesting to him, it was in reverse formation, with the Class 91 Electra trailing. Undaunted, he caught the following train for Glasgow, intending to get off at Waverley and find his dad.

Unfortunately, for what the guard described as "operational reasons", it didn't stop at Edinburgh Waverley, or Haymarket, but headed straight for Glasgow. Johnny Junior noticed that, unusually, it took the southerly route, via Uddingston, thus arriving into Glasgow Central, not Queen Street. He wasn't too worried as it was an opportunity to do more trainspotting, and for lots more photos. It would have helped, he realised, if Dad was a bit more in touch with the modern world, like having a mobile phone.

Meanwhile Johnny was deep in conversation with a young lady at the Information Desk on Waverley's main concourse. Listening carefully, she checked her screen.

"I think I know what's happened", she said. "Your son caught the delayed 09.25 Berwick-Glasgow train. That service didn't stop here, so he'll be in Glasgow."

"Aye, trainspotting, no doubt. with no idea of the time, or the trouble he's in. I'd best get over there and look for him."

He just made the 11.00 departure from Platform 14.

Meanwhile Johnny Junior, having had a similar conversation at Glasgow Queen Street, caught the 11.00 for Edinburgh.

Although their carriages stopped alongside in Falkirk High, they didn't see each other. Johnny Junior was too busy looking out for the Flying Banana, Network Rail's special new measurement train. Johnny, fast asleep, was dreaming of wedding breakfasts in Brechin.

Back at Waverley, Johnny Junior made his way to the information desk, and the very same young lady. She saw the family likeness immediately.

"Your dad's gone to Glasgow Queen Street to find you. Looks like he'll no' be in luck."

Johnny Junior decided to head back to Berwick, as the guard had told him the Flying Banana would overnight in the station siding. It was later that day that father and son were re-united, not altogether happily although Johnny Junior wasn't too upset. He'd got some extra trainspotting, and, even better, his dad said he wouldn't have to go to Brechin after all.

Johnny, however, was more determined than ever. Next morning, he was back on the 09.30 to Waverley. He'd decided to stop off in Edinburgh to visit the Scott Monument in Prince's Street; and pick up the 14.25

for Montrose, the nearest station to Brechin. Now, as you may know, the platform configuration at Edinburgh Waverley appears eccentric. For example, Platform 19 is the western section of Platform 2, which is the eastern section of Platform 19. Likewise, Platform 20 is the western section of Platform 1, and vice versa. But there is a logic to it, which becomes apparent if you think of a clock with Platform 1 closest to the Balmoral Hotel at 1.0 o'clock. The rest follow clockwise back to Platform 20 at the equivalent of 11.0 o'clock.

Johnny, like most, was unaware of this. Arriving at Waverley in good time he checked the departure boards and made his way towards Platform 19, for the 14.25 for Aberdeen, calling at Haymarket, Dundee, Arbroath, Montrose, and Stonehaven. He thought Platform 19 would be one long platform. Except that it isn't.

So, when he turned right instead of left, he was surprised to find a red carpet leading to the Highland Clansman, most luxurious of trains. A kilted bagpiper with an unconvincing false moustache skirled the Skye Boat Song, and two charming young ladies welcomed Johnny aboard, escorting him to his very plush seat. He noticed the letters HC embroidered on the antimacassar. Peering around at his fellow passengers, they looked important. But then, he told himself, he was important, thinking "Do you know, Johnny m'lad, this travel business is surprisingly enjoyable after all. No wonder everyone's up to 'Leave'. Clearly Brechin is the place to be."

They had barely passed through Haymarket when the drinks trolley came round, and everyone was a given a "Welcome Aboard the Whisky Wanderer" leaflet. Getting into the spirit, Johnny treated himself to a wee dram. Two, actually. Gliding past the airport on his magic carpet, he felt himself wafted across the Forth on the magnificent railway bridge.

The Highland Clansman slid through the Fife countryside like a dream. Occasional announcements heralded places of interest close by: the Palace of Falkirk, the Hill of Tarvit, and the infamous Tay Bridge. Johnny thought that, after Dundee, they would follow the east coast. They didn't. Instead, they turned west, through Perth, then south, to Gleneagles. Here the bagpiper appeared on the platform again, without his false moustache this time, but accompanied by a thickset, slightly menacing looking golfer in traditional garb – tartan plus-fours, check waistcoat, flat cap, and a hickory driver. They invited Johnny and fellow guests (they were paying far too much to be mere passengers) to a few holes, a round even. If this seemed too strenuous, and for most it did, there was a lecture about the hotel and its famous past. Johnny listened with interest, but also mild concern. He had expected that, after Dundee, they would head north to Montrose. Surely there was a distillery there too? Or was it at Brechin?

Returning to the train after dinner at Gleneagles, Johnny turned to a tour hostess, a young lady from Asia with limited English. She looked askance.

"Montrose? No sir, not on Whisky Wanderer. Next stop Stirling, in morning, we take tour of ancient distillery near Alloa. Now, we all shunting up siding for night. I tell you, sir, most guests pretty ready for bunking soon."

"Brechin? "Johnny enquired.

"Bunking, sir. Sleeping in bunk. I make up. You like nightcap?"

"No, not bunking…Brechin?"

"Sorry sir, I not understanding."

"Brexit, perhaps?" Johnny asked hopefully.

"Yes, sir, breakfast! " She jumped on the word with relief. "In dining car, eighty thirty on dot. Fully scrambled Scottish salmon with wild eggs. Or continental, with very nice fresh Dutch bakers."

Johnny, bemused, realised he was tired. He hadn't had so much excitement for a long time. Probably since that wedding breakfast in Brechin.

"Time to board train, sir, I show you cabin. You looking like you need good long shut-eye."

Johnny had strange dreams that night, in the siding at Gleneagles. In one a Victorian gentleman appeared, wearing a tartan top hat, holding a hickory driver in one hand and a ragged copy of a newspaper in the other.

"Hello Johnny m'lad, Wilson's the name. John Wilson, erstwhile editor of the Berwick Advertiser, until I got the call, rather unexpectedly early, I always thought, back in 1835. I do hope you're enjoying your trip. It's not quite what young Leighton had in mind, but he wrote a ripping yarn alright. I'll be intrigued to see how you go on, now that humankind has moved on from stage- coaches and sailing..."

Next morning he was wakened by loud knocking on the cabin door. It was the bagpiper, still sans moustache.

"Sorry to bother you, but you're Johnny Armstrong from Berwick-upon-Tweed aren't you?"

"The same, and have been for the past sixty-five, years, two months and, let me see now," he looked down at his watch, "eight days."

"I'm Jamie McDougall. Son of Hamish."

"My old friend Hamish eh? God rest his soul. Yes, I can see the likeness now, especially when you're not wearing that comic moustache. It really didn't suit you."

"I wondered if we might breakfast together, before the tour of the distillery. I hear that the tour organisers are going to announce a change of plan, a special surprise."

"So long as it gets me to Brechin, I'll be happy."

"Brechin? Funny you should mention it. My maiden aunt Clarissa lives there. All the men fell for her when she was young. Still do, I'm told."

Johnny turned pale and sat down. That young lady he had kissed. Her name was Clarissa.

The surprise wasn't only a complimentary bottle of malt whisky, although that was welcome. It was a luxury coach ride down to the docks at Rosyth. There, towering above them, grey and menacing, the pride-to-be of the British Navy, state-of-the-art aircraft carrier HMS Prince of Wales, being prepared for launching in 2017. Nearby the Highland Duchess, a luxury cruise ship, looked tiny. Apparently there'd been some hiccup with the train, so the Whisky Wanderer was taking its esteemed guests up the Firth of Forth and to sea for the next leg, up the coast to Aberdeen. Unfortunately Johnny and Jamie never made it off the coach. Sprawled the length of the back seat, an empty bottle of malt between them, it was only when the coach driver got back to the depot in Arbroath that he heard loud snoring.

Arbroath's Pickled Smokie was a quayside watering hole popular with fishermen and sailors. Our two friends found themselves inexorably drawn to it. There they fell in with the crew of the Vertipaxi Sunrise, sister ship of Vertipaxi Sunset, on a research trip around Scotland, measuring levels of plastic pollution. One round led to another, as they do, although Johnny had half an eye on the news-feed on the television above the bar. Muted, sub-titles turned on. It flagged up "Breaking News", then "Brexit Bombshell", then, surprisingly, "Brechin Bonanza". More than one over the eight by then, he struggled to recall something important. It slid from his consciousness. Half walking, half carried, he was barely aware of the quayside drifting along beside him before he passed out.

Aboard the Vertipaxi Sunrise, Johnny was wakened from uneasy slumber several hours later by the roaring wind, the splashing, dashing, gurly waves, a commotion on deck, and Jamie, who was in the upper bunk, informing him that they were heading out towards the Bell Rock lighthouse. Landlubbers both, they weren't at ease on the briny, especially with the wind whipping itself up the Beaufort scale to Force 10. Worse, the steering gear had jammed. Rudderless, the Vertipaxi Sunrise found herself not just heading for the Bell Rock but aground on it. So undignified.

In the old days the crew would have been winched to safety by the lighthouse keepers. Not now, because the Bell Rock light is unmanned and operated remotely from Trinity House HQ.

Luckily there was a gas drilling rig nearby. The riggers, spotting their plight, sent a rigid inflatable boat over. But the Vertipaxi Sunrise crew were determined to stay aboard, fix the rudder, and re-float on the next high tide. Truth to tell, they didn't appreciate landlubbers on board, especially not a half-cut Englishman, or a Scottish bagpiper. A few minutes later, Johnny and Jamie were hoisted unceremoniously aboard

the rig. To Johnny's horror it turned out to be Dutch, with no one speaking much English. When he tried to explain that he was hoping to get to Brechin, they looked blank.

"Freakin? Fracking? Breaking?".

"No, not breaking", said Johnny, exasperated. "Brechin. B-R-E-C-H-I-N! Over there, in Scotland."

He pointed west. One rigger thought he understood.

"Ah man, now I get you. Brexit! You no want Brexit? You like go Dutch? Hello, yes, you very welcome. Helicopter leave in one hour. We fly very quick. Holland very close."

Smiling broadly, he pointed east and gave Johnny a whack on the shoulders. Sea-leg-less, he keeled over.

Picking himself off the deck, Johnny tried in vain to explain that he wanted to go back to Scotland. The mainland, tantalisingly, appeared, disappeared and re-appeared through the spume. The helicopter pilot promised to fly Johnny to Rotterdam, where he knew an excellent hostelry, so that he could sort out becoming a Dutch national. Jamie, meanwhile, kept busy tuning his bagpipes, worried that they might have taken in seawater. He refused to budge, saying that he was afraid of flying, and asking if they had any whisky on board.

The Dutch immigration authorities tracked Johnny down in the Fisherman's Rest a run down dorpscafe near the docks in Rotterdam. As he had no passport or papers with him, the official had no option but to classify him an illegal immigrant, explaining that he would be deported to the UK, booked on the next ferry from Zeebrugge to Rosyth. Surprised at Johnny's delight, he looked bemused. Crazy English.

"You want Brexit? No like Europe?"

"Brechin" said Johnny. "Me, I like Brechin..." Would nobody ever understand?

Now Johnny might have been fine on the regular lorry, commercial vehicle and container ferry from Zeebrugge to Rosyth, except that, on checking in, he was informed by the young lady on the desk that he was a truckless trucker. Luckily he didn't mishear, and took this on the chin.

A kindly soul, she arranged for a colleague to drive him to Ijmuiden to pick up the regular passenger ferry to North Shields, and thence to Newcastle Central, and an East Coast train to Berwick-upon-Tweed, where Johnny Junior met him at the station.

"Hi Dad, great to see you. Guess what I've just seen - the Flying Banana."

"Well done laddie, and yes, good to see you too. Everything OK?"

"All fine, Dad, nothing much to report, just a message from someone called Jamie. He told me you last saw him playing his bagpipes on a gas rig near the Bell Rock. What on earth were you doing out there?"

"It's a long story, I'll tell you later. The message?"

"He's been to Brechin, to see his maiden aunt Clarissa. She'd like you to get in touch. Something about Brexit apparently."

Retold by Nick Jones

The Disasters of Johnny Armstrong companion piece

The Disasters of Johnny Armstrong was written by Alexander Campbell who wrote forty of Wilson's tales. Although it was not the fifth tale published in the weekly magazine, this tale was the fifth tale in Volume 1 – which probably means it was collected in 1834 or written before that volume was published and Wilson dying the following year.

What was happening in, say the early decades of the century, regarding public transport? Since it is the author's story and not that of later generations, here I must correct Nick Jones' setting of Johnny Armstrong's domicile. Johnny lived in Carlisle not Berwick – though why spoil a good story by Nick? Campbell would have known the stagecoach movements in Carlisle so let us stick to that for the moment.

The Regency period was the golden age of the stagecoach, until the railways displaced them to a great extent after the 1830s. After two centuries of bumping discomfort the vehicles were now becoming better sprung and the incredible speed of 12 miles per hour could be expected. Johnny and Johnny Junior in real life would have probably departed Carlisle from the old Crown and Mitre coffee house run by a Mrs Sarah Alkin which was demolished in 1902 – the present day inn dates from 1905. The new "fast mail" to Glasgow was initiated in 1832 – I suspect this was not around when Johnny Junior was whisked off. Incidentally the "fast mail" was expected to travel at about 11 mph and changed horses every six miles. Presumably the slow mail did not cause "the passengers to expire through lack of oxygen."

In those days the distances by road from Carlisle were – Edinburgh, 91 miles, Glasgow 104 miles, Dumfries 40 miles.

Thomas Telford's construction of the Carlisle to Glasgow road (now the A74) might account for the breakneck speed of 11 mph. The following coaches may have been used by the Armstrongs: the Glasgow stage left the coffee house at 3pm via Ecclefechan, Lockerbie, Moffat, Elvanfoot, Douglas-mill, and Hamilton, arriving at Smart's Hotel in Glasgow at around 8am the following day. It then returned at 3pm and arrived in Carlisle at 8am the next day. The fare was £1.15s, but travelling on the coach roof would have been much cheaper. A few years later it may have been the Independent to Glasgow, every day, Sundays excepted, at 3.30pm via Annan, Dumfries, Kilmarnock and Lanark, returning at 10pm.

The Portpatrick mail coach which served Dumfries set out every day from the coffee house, via Longtown and Annan, at three o'clock in the afternoon, and arrived at The George, Dumfries at ten o'clock the same night, the landlady being a Mrs McVitie. It then set out from the same inn about nine o'clock at night, and arrived at the coffee house, Carlisle, at three o'clock in the morning of the following day. The fare from Carlisle to Dumfries was 13s. Note the departure times of the Glasgow stage and the Portpatrick (Dumfries) stage both between 3pm and 3.30pm – this would account for Johnny's confusion.

The Independent to Edinburgh, every Monday Wednesday and Friday at 5am, ran through Longtown, Langholm and Hawick returning to Carlisle on Tuesday, Thursday and Saturday at 6pm. The Sir Walter Scott to Edinburgh, ran every Monday, Wednesday and Friday morning at 4.30am, through Langholm, Hawick, and Selkirk, returning at 6pm.

London coaches set out from the King's Arms as well as the coffee house. The principal inns in Carlisle were The Bush, in English St, kept by Fairburn - also in English street the King's Arms, by Hardesty; the Coffee-house, by Alkin, Castle St, The Grapes Inn, by Pringle, and the Duke's Head by Sowerby were in Scotch St. There were other less salubrious hostelries of course.

The 35 mile long Forth and Clyde canal was opened in 1790. The Armstrongs would have been passengers on one of the steam boats introduced from 1805. They did the run from Edinburgh to Glasgow in six to seven hours and provided refreshments, newspapers and of course glorious scenery for travellers.

In the early years of the 19th century ferries were almost all powered by wind or oarsmen but around the time of our tale a revolution was taking place. The steamboat ferries across the Forth from Newhaven harbour ran to Dysart near Kirkcaldy from September 1819. They were known as the Broad Ferry and took away much of the business of the Queensferry crossing which, due to currents and tides was at that time not viable for steam ferries. Because of the uncertain dating of the tale, we don't know what the author had in mind. Of course the Alloa ferry runs in the opposite direction – upriver, hence Johnny's problem. There is little doubt, reinforced by Johnny's encounter with the engineer, that he travelled on a steamboat.

The nightmare voyage to Montrose which ended in Holland and the mistaken arrest of Johnny causes us a slight problem in discovering the date to which the tale relates. From 1793 to 1815, with a short break to get their breath back, Britain was at war with France and for most of the time with Holland (Batavian Republic), so presumably the tale is set after 1815 with a slight possibility of the Peace of Amiens in 1802-3. Further on in the tale we find an interesting clue. The author/narrator says "as we were strolling down the pier of Leith, with a friend, one afternoon in 18—" (a frustrating missing two digits) – " we saw a vessel making for the harbour..." and he goes on to describe witnessing Johnny's return.

Alexander Campbell, the author of 40 of Wilson's tales, wrote a later story "The Snow Storm of 1825" so I think we can opt for a date after 1815 for this tale. Technically I should say 1814 because the Batavian Republic had surrendered in that year before Napoleon escaped from Elba and after "The Hundred Days" his career ended at Waterloo.

The 91 miles frantic hay cart ride from Edinburgh could have been avoided if Johnny had taken advantage of one of the regular goods carriers from Edinburgh. We see from the Carlisle trade directory that John Hislop & Son and John McIntosh, from Edinburgh, would arrive at "Mrs Beck's and James Nixon's"; Hislop, on Tuesday and Friday, returning Saturday and Wednesday; McIntosh, on Fridays and returning the next day.

One of the fascinating things about Wilson's tales is the patchy information available now as to the identity of some of the authors. The tales were for the main part undated and give no personal details about authors. Perhaps this is an area of rewarding research for the project. I tried to fit the following author to the tale but probably came unstuck when I found he had died in 1824 and that he appears to have written a story set in 1825. I leave you to judge from the following notes:

A man called Alexander Campbell was the writer of miscellaneous works, an organist, a qualified, though probably non-practising, surgeon, born near Loch Lubnaig in Perthshire in 1764 and, like Wilson, perpetually short of money. Campbell died in 1824 so perhaps Wilson had the tales from a collection of unpublished work sold "under judicial authority" after his death? Campbell was not considered a great writer but this tale was obviously a worthy addition to Wilson's tales.

Background by Michael Oliver

The Maiden Feast of Cairnkibbie

King James V had a reputation for good-humoured eccentricity and love of fun. He also enjoyed incognito trips among his subjects, getting a reputation as a prince of good fellows and the unofficial title "King of the Commons." His riding, shooting and swordplay skills were as well known as his expertise in dancing, music and his ability to tell a good yarn. In short, an all-round good chap.

Now James was in the "auld burgh" of Duns with his lords, including the Lord of Ross. Knowing of all these attributes Ross issued a detailed challenge to the king in the form of a wager. It was that James should dress as a beggar and gate crash one of the Maiden feasts held on farms to celebrate the end of harvest. There he must try to win the hearts of all present so that they would defend him against all comers. Ross even specified that the merrymakers must be prepared to take arms against the king's own knights rather than give the beggar over to justice if he was accused of a crime. Furthermore, he would have to steal a valuable horse, escape from capture and return to Duns.

James accepted what looked like an impossible challenge, determined to win the day by disguising himself as a gaberlunzie, one of the licensed beggars of the time. Under the "auld rights o' the gaberlunzies of Scotland" these beggars were entitled to enter a Maiden feast to dance, drink and kiss all the lassies. Hung about with the traditional gaberlunzie's wallet, "sundry appendages" and his pipes James set off to lord it amongst his people as Wat Wilson, "King of the Beggars."

Near Foulden on the Whiteadder river, harvest had been safely gathered in at a farm called Cairnkibbie, the final ears of corn woven into the propitiatory maiden and the feast underway. And what a feast! The merry makers, unaware of the approaching royal roysterer, were kicking up their heels in energetic reels, presided over by the farmer, guidman William Hume, his "sleek and comfortable guidwife" and his bonny daughter, Lilly.

The guests had come from far and wide dressed in their best, creating a colourful scene filled with the spirit of the Maiden feast. Their 'Tam Lutar', the blind piper of the feast, played his heart out, particularly when his efforts were oiled by the good ale beside him, from a vessel topped up whenever the dancers felt that the piper was flagging.

Although Lilly was considered a lady on account of her father's status she danced with all, even the "humblest hind," showing her to be a generous- hearted lassie. But her outward cheerfulness hid secret sorrow. She loved Will Carr but her father had refused to allow them to dance together. That seemed strange. Will was handsome, he came of a good family, he had a "gentle demeanour" and was considered by all to be a "decent callant". The love between the two had grown during secret meetings "amongst the broom knowes of Cairnkibbie". So what was William Hume's objection? In a word: poverty. William Hume would never allow his daughter to marry a poverty-stricken suitor.

Despite these hidden tensions the fun at the feast grew fast and furious. There were riotous reels as dancers whirled around while those exhausted by the dancing took themselves into secluded corners for the refreshment found in bottles and on willing lips.

Suddenly an argument started between Will Aitken and Jock Hedderwick, harsh words rising above the music and singing. The gaberlunzie had arrived. Would the "auld rights" apply? Would the gaberlunzie be entitled to enter this Maiden feast to dance and drink and kiss the lassies? Jock Hedderwick would have none of it while Will Aitken was a traditionalist with his argument centred on the ancient laws of hospitality. Such laws were sacred, he argued, and he was able to convince the company that the "pawky auld carle" with his pipes and wallets should be admitted. Lilly promptly opened the door. The cat among the pigeons indeed.

The gaberlunzie unleashed his charm on the company. There he stood, with his bags and baggage, raising the rafters with his laughter, moving around the company slapping men on their backs and kissing the girls. Will Carr brought him ale and the gaberlunzie was quick to spot Will's sadness. He noted the exchange of glances between the two lovers and, sensitive to this sour note in the festivities, demanded more ale from a fresh barrel as his right.

His capacity for drink was astonishing. No sooner had he finished one drink than he demanded another, stating that he needed lubrication as he intended to take the place of the blind piper. His piping proved so stirring that, although the dancers were weary, they set to with renewed zest.

Despite his lively playing the king was still aware of the tension between Lilly and Will Carr. Puzzled, he managed during a pause to get a confession from Lilly that her father had forbidden them to dance. When tasked for the reason, Lilly's reply was succinct, "He's puir."

The king's reaction? An acknowledgement that poverty is a "red crime... If he had killed a score o' God's creatures in a Border raid, he micht hae been forgi'en. But wha forgies poverty?"

Determined that the couple should dance together, James recalled Tam, the blind piper to play "The Hunts o' Cheviot" while he formed a set with Lilly as his partner and blushing Bess Gordon as Will's. The dance proved both noisy and infectious and even Lilly's parents joined in. Tam piped, the dancers called out their "Hough! Houghs!" and merriment prevailed. James achieved his aim of bringing the lovers together by waiting for the moment when the parents' backs were turned. He switched from Lilly to Bess as his partner, encouraging Will to give Lilly a kiss and a "good squeeze o' her hand."

Calling for Tam to play "King William's Note" he inspired the company to greater heights of dancing and made a point of kissing "lug to lug" every damsel in the place, including Lilly's mother. When the dancing eventually ended he sang and told tales to delight the company further. By now he was a universal favourite, acknowledged by the name he had given them, Wat Wilson. He was, indeed, the king of the feast and having gained the hearts of all there he had won part of his wager with the Lord of Ross.

But what of the rest of the wager? Just when mirth was at its height and all under the sway of the beggar king, there was the sound of horses. The king's knights entered, claiming that this gaberlunzie was a common thief who had stolen the silver mace of King James. Drama indeed.

Argument was fast and furious with charges from the knights and denials from the disguised king. These accusations, however, were subtle compliments as they praised the king's athletic prowess. One knight stated that the beggar ran faster than a greyhound, a compliment backed by William Hume who testified to the energy displayed in the beggar's dancing: "If our friend ran as cleverly as he has danced this night, a' the greyhounds o' the Merse wadna hae catched him." Without knowing it, William Hume was finding favour with the king.

A demand that the beggar be given up to justice provoked instant opposition from William Hume and the whole company. It became obvious to the knights that all the men there were prepared to fight for this charismatic beggar even if armed only with their farming tools. The Lord of Ross scented the loss of his wager.

When a search for the missing mace was organised, the beggar himself took out the object from his wallet, held it up and claimed it as his "badge" as Wat Wilson, "king o' the beggars, crowned on Hogmanay, on the Warlock's Hill near Duns." He challenged the knights to take it from him.

The "foremost knight" made a direct appeal to William Hume, inviting him to inspect the mace and warning him of the charge of high treason which would be levelled, not only at the beggar but also those who sheltered him. He said, "James will punish thee…" knowing as he, and all the knights knew, that James was standing there gleefully appreciating the situation. It was a testing time for William Hume. What would he do?

In his reply, William showed his true colours as a bold, brave man. He acknowledged the laws of hospitality when he claimed the beggar as "Our guest" and, with innocent irony, went on to say: "King Jamie himself is nae mair like the king o' this auld land, than this jolly gaberlunzie is like the king o' his tribe… He sings like a king, dances like a king, drinks like a king, and kisses the lasses like a king - and, king as he is, feth we'll be his loyal subjects." All this must have been music to James' ears and the Lord of Ross would have recognised the loss of yet another part of his wager.

There was only one answer to such blatant opposition - a "Battle Royal." In the ensuing melee the women were manoeuvred out the back door while the knights, determined not to shed blood, focused on trying to capture the beggar. The beggar was equally determined not to be caught as he still had part of the wager to accomplish - the imprisoning of the knights and his escape and return to Duns. To that end he directed the operation with "great adroitness and spirit." As a result of his efforts the knights found themselves locked in a dark barn with no means of escape. The beggar celebrated his victory with a triumphal pibroch, his pipes drowning out the roars of the knights coming through the door. With cutting irony he shouted, "Ye may tell yer king…that he is not the only king in these realms. And surely Scotland is wide enough for twa…Wat Wilson's no' the potentate that wad ever interfere wi' Jamie Stuart, if Jamie Stuart will let alane Wat Wilson." Thus his claim to be not only their king, but truly "The King of the Commons."

William Hume by then was pot-valiant as he had taken good ale aplenty. He was, however, aware enough to be puzzled as to why the confined knights had become so quiet and seemed to have "submitted to their durance like lambs in a sheepfold." When he asked the beggar about this mystery the beggar's laughing reply "attributed the quietness and meekness of the foes to the terror of his prowess, and the awe which his name inspired throughout a great part of Scotland."

Poor old William, sobering up, recognised his predicament and realised that they had been led astray by the personal magnetism of "a wanderin' beggar." He decided he would discuss the situation with the gaberlunzie and release the king's men as an act of prudence, only to find that the beggar had disappeared, riding away in the moonlight on one of the king's horses complete with his wallet, pipes and the stolen mace.

The seriousness of William's position was now clear and the feast seemed as a dream. William blamed the beggar, but also himself. He was in a cleft stick. If the knights were released William and his men could all be slaughtered. But the longer the knights were confined the worse things could become. A deal had to be made: the knights would be freed so long as there were no killings and an amnesty would be requested for the loss of the horse.

In bargaining with the knights, William blamed his predicament on the beggar who he claimed was the devil himself. To the amazement of the feast-goers, the response from the knights was laughter. The prisoners seemed "right merry" and even roared with laughter when William told them that the beggar had stolen "the best horse o'a' yer cavalcade." There was a tense moment when the bolts were withdrawn, but there was nothing but good will all round with the released prisoners slapping the bemused William on the back and demanding a return of the dancing.

Deciding there was a time and a place for everything, William held up his hands and decided that moralising could wait. Festivities were renewed. But, alas, the zest for them had gone with the gaberlunzie. He had been an "Arab steed" compared with the "plough nags" of the knights. He was like a comet which blazed briefly in splendour, then left them in darkness. With his absence the glory had gone. And so ended the Maiden feast. The knights rode off and William and his wife went to bed.

But! Came the dawn- came the king's messenger with a schedule of charges against William. One- he had given refuge and protection to the thieving gaberlunzie. Two- he had defended the thief against the king's men. Three- "he did pummel and lik in a shameful manner the same men." Four-he had imprisoned the same men so enabling the gaberlunzie to escape on the "choisest" horse. This schedule of charges was under the king's signature and William was summoned to answer them at "the present ambulatory court" in Duns.

The book had been thrown at William Hume. He did not know what to do. But the messenger was sympathetic and, with an eye on bonny Lilly, he advised William to take her with him to court because "the king cannot resist the appeal of beauty."

A day and a night of torment followed for the whole family. In loyalty to William his wife, Lilly, Will Carr and some of the servants decided they would accompany him. After a deal of debate William decided that his best defence was simply to tell the truth. They travelled to Duns, dressed in their best, where they were met by the king's officers and conducted to a fine room usually used as a garrison for troops.

The room alone filled the party with awe, but more awe-inspiring was the king seated on an elevated throne with the Scots' lords at his feet. Although feeling like a fish out of water, once on his feet to answer the charges William gained confidence. He claimed that the gaberlunzie was "neither mair nor less than his august Majesty was..."

Dramatic pause. King and lords thought momentarily that William had recognised the gaberlunzie and Jamie as one and the same. "He knows him, he knows him," was the whisper amongst the laughing lords. But William's hesitation was because he was deliberating whether or not to claim the gaberlunzie as the Devil. When he did so the lords were delighted and claimed the charge as a compliment to the king. William was so innocent that he was unable to put two and two together and realise that the beggar was no other than the king of Scotland.

When the king demanded what it was that the beggar had actually done, William's list of qualities must have been music to his ears. Even the greatest love admiration and the lords needed to know what happened before their arrival at the feast so that the terms of the wager could be met.

William's list included the beggar's ability to turn enemies into friends, skill in playing, dancing, kissing, singing like a "bullfinch" and generally inspiring by his "glamour and witchery o' fun and frolic." One more quality which William ascribed to the "enemy," by which he meant the devil, was "a luve o' himself," a hint at the self-centredness that underlay James's play-acting.

William made it clear that only the devil could have inspired what happened at the Maiden and he summed up his defence with the plea "Could a beggar o' ordinary flesh and blude hae dune a' that, yer Highness?" That was, unknown to William the innocent, another compliment to the king as having near superhuman qualities, even invisibility when the horse was stolen.

While poor William and his family and friends waited in agony for the outcome of his defence the king and Ross whispered together, the king claiming he had won the wager and Ross laughing and admitting defeat: "Your Highness has won the day."

But the Humes' torment was not yet over as the king declared he was leaving to "put on the black cap," claiming that William's words were simply "an artifice on thy part to escape vengeance." The family's reactions to that only gave more merriment to lords who seemed to revel in causing misery. When the king returned wearing the "cap of Wat Wilson and holding in his hand the stolen mace," the penny eventually dropped and "the fears of all were in a moment dispelled." Having accused William of artifice the king's own deception was revealed.

The outcome ? There had to be some reward for the hapless Humes although the king's absolute power was first revealed as he overruled William's objection to a match between Lilly and Will Carr. William was amazed that the king knew of Will Carr's poverty as he and his wife had never let this objection be known because Will's people "canna help their poverty." Lilly herself was so overcome by the grandeur of her surroundings that she uttered not a word, so the king could only ask William directly if he still opposed the match. What could William do but withdraw his opposition as the king himself "gies the bans."

Then came the rewards. William was to be given "free grant" of the lands of Cairnkibbie, changing him from farmer to a small Border laird, on condition that he allowed the union of the lovers. Will Carr was rewarded with 200 marks from the royal purse; a rags-to-riches ending. The involvement of the king and his presence at the Maiden feast was to be kept a secret. Will and Lilly were married and another feast took place - but this time without the gaberlunzie.

Retold by Christine Fletcher

The Maiden Feast of Cairnkibbie companion piece

The central themes of "The Maiden Feast of Cairnkibbie" are trust, loyalty, friendship and in particular, the true meaning of wealth. The last is an enduring theme that in modern culture is explored in books such as, The Prince and The Pauper, films like Trading Places, and notably the "reality" television programme, The Secret Millionaire.

A "maiden", according to the Dictionary of Scots Language is, "The last bunch of corn to be cut on a particular farm at harvest time, frequently shaped and decorated in the image of a maiden and regarded as a symbol of the corn spirit. Hence, by extension: the harvest-home feast and celebrations." In medieval Britain as elsewhere, a harvest was a time of anticipation and worry: the months leading up to it might have been a time of hunger as grain stores emptied and Lammas Day—"loaf mass"—1 August, traditionally the first day of the harvest was a noted time of celebration anticipating better times. The main harvest festival coincided with the harvest moon of the autumn equinox. Indeed, "harvest" is from the Old English word hærfest, meaning "autumn".

Whether actual or fictional, Cairnkibbie a typical Merse farm near Foulden, Berwickshire would have been instantly recognised by any reader of "The Tales", or indeed by anyone from the time it is set in—probably the 1530s—during the short reign of James V of Scotland (1513–42).

A stranger, the gaberlunzie[1], who claims to be Wat Wilson, King of Beggars, comes amidst the celebrations of the Cairnkibbie farm and is treated with suspicion, only to win the trust and friendship of the merry-makers to the point of their defending him against the king's soldiers—a seemingly insuperable task.

The next morning, the guidman—the farmer William Hume—regrets his actions of the previous night, especially when he is summonsed to appear before the king, and pleads his actions were the will of the Devil and hopes his honesty will save the day.

King James V ascended the throne at the age of 17 months after the death of his father at Flodden in 1513. After a spell of imprisonment for his "safety", he finally took control of the throne in 1528. According to legend he was known as the "King of the Commons" as he would sometimes travel around Scotland disguised as a common man, describing himself as the "Guidman of Ballengeich" ("Ballengeich" was the nickname of a road next to Stirling Castle.)

James was a cultured man, a keen lutenist, and most interestingly, a poet. Among his (supposed) works the two best known are of interest to us: "The Gaberlunzie Man"[2] and "The Jolly Beggar"[3] telling the tales of beggars who, by cunning "steal" a farmer's daughter. The author of "The Maiden Feast of Cairnkibbie", Alexander Leighton, published a 20 part, 10 volume publication of the collected "Tales" in 1857. The two purportedly royal writings were published in the 18th century and so were likely to have been known to him, and possibly, to inspire him. However, beggars often featured in morality tales long before the ballads became popular in print form.

Ane Pleasant Satyre of the Thrie Estaitis, is a satirical morality play in Middle Scots, written by makar Sir David Lyndsay, first performed in June 1552 The Satire is an attack on the Three Estates represented in the Parliament of Scotland—the clergy, lords and burgh representatives, symbolised by the characters Spiritualitie, Temporalitie and Merchant.

The critic John MacQueen proposed the play might have been composed by Lindsay as early as 1532 for the court of the young James V of Scotland. An early form of the play is recorded in the royal treasurer's accounts and an English agent's report to Thomas Cromwell. This short play or "interlude" performed in January 1540 used characters who later appeared in the Satyre of the Thrie Estaitis, and had the same themes. A Poor Man complains about the justice meted to him when on the scaffold and is answered by a Burgess, a Man at Arms and a Bishop, who represented the three estates of the Parliament of Scotland. Essentially, it is a critique, mainly of the church in Scotland. This was the time of the Reformation in England and although he was known not to tolerate heresy, it is said that after the performance James asked the clergymen present to reform their treatment of the poor. What caused James to disguise himself as a pauper and go amidst the multitude, can only be guessed at. Was it an uncertain childhood, or perhaps the knowledge his father was slain by a common soldier and died in the mud of Flodden with so many of his countrymen? Perhaps it was just common decency.

Of course, one can as any Victorian writer might, look to the Bible for inspiration. Two stories stand out. The parable of a rich man, Dives, and a poor beggar named Lazarus (Luke 16:19–31) tells of their relationship before and after death. In life, Lazarus has nothing and dies at the rich man's gate for want of food but is admitted to heaven, while the rich man who had everything on earth ends up in hell. The parable of the judgment (Matthew 25:31-46) connects to the Sermon on the Mount because it shows the importance of right attitude leading to right charitable action. Some people who receive salvation will be surprised because they did not personally follow Jesus, but supported his believers and helped Christ in this way.

One can also draw upon the medieval cult of memento mori: "remember that you too must die". It has, in many religions been a means of perfecting the character by cultivating detachment and other virtues, and by turning the attention towards the immortality of the soul and the afterlife. In other words, we all look the same in the grave.

Another character from literature that may have inspired Leighton is Prince Hal in Shakespeare's Henry IV part I. The future Henry V spends his time in bawdy taverns in the company of Falstaff and his band of rogues, supposedly to find out how the common man lives, although of course it may be as much for his own entertainment as alternate princely education, and in the end he is seen to denounce Falstaff.

In this play, Falstaff insults his friend Bardolph referencing the tale of Dives and Lazarus: "I never see thy face, but I think upon hell-fire and Dives that lived in purple; for there he is in his robes, burning, burning" (III, 3, 30–33), and the death of Falstaff is compared to that of Lazarus in Henry V (II.3,7–8).

And so, in the "The Maiden...," King James is seen, by facing his relatively poorer countryman with the moral dilemma—what is the value of a man's life?—to demonstrate to his court, and himself, that underneath the trappings of wealth, we are all equal. Although the gaberlunzie is poor in appearance and wealth, he more than makes up for it with his ability to sing, dance and play the pipes, such that even when his identity is revealed as the King, his presence is sorely missed at the wedding that follows. Thus he brought a value to the Hume household more than money could buy. The theme's emphasis of relative wealth is furthered, when the King confronts Hume who regards the poorer Will Carr as not good enough for Lilly Hume.

At the end of the "The Maiden..." all ends well: Hume and Carr are rewarded for showing charity and kindness, as taught by the parable of the judgment, as should we all.

Cairnhill Engraving from 1934 Edition

References

Leighton, Alexander: Wilson's Tales of the Borders and of Scotland, Vol IV (1885). Source: http://www.gutenberg.org/files/34144/34144-h/34144-h.htm#THE_MAIDEN_FEAST_OF_CAIRNKIBBIE

Dictionary of the Scots Language Source: http://www.dsl.ac.uk

http://www.contemplator.com/child/gaberlunz.html

Eyre-Todd, George, 1892: Scottish Poetry of the Sixteenth Century, pp176–182. Source: https://archive.org/details/scottishpoetryof00eyre

Wikipedia—various

[1] Gaberlunzie: An ancient Scots name for a hawker, from gaber, "a wallet", and lunzie, "the loin". Literally, "The man who carries a wallet on the loin."

Originally, the "z" was a yogh, with the consonant sound of "y", (written ꝫ). Typographic laziness replaced the "long z" with the ordinary character. This peculiarity is preserved to the present day in several Scottish proper names, such as Dalziel and Culzean.

[2] The Gaberlunzie Man appears in a ballad sheet "The Original Comic Song Book: New songs by Thomas Ramsay". It was to be sung to the tune John Highland Man. "The Gaberlunzie Man" appears in Ramsay's Tea Table Miscellany in 1724.

Child includes the ballad "The Gaberlunzie Man" as an appendix to Child Ballad #279 "The Jolly Beggar". He states the tradition that ascribes it to James V does not date earlier than the appearance of the ballad in 1724.

[3] "The Jolly Beggar" is cited in Percy's Reliques of Ancient English Poetry (1767) and appears in Herd (1769). A broadside ballad "The Pollitick Begger-Man" was entered in the Stationers' Register(1656). It has substantially the same story, and was probably the basis for this Scottish ballad.

Background by Jim Herbert

The Shoes Reversed

Between green and peaceful banks the River Liddel flows from the Cheviot Hills westward. The stream is all which a pastoral stream should ever aspire to: neither turbid nor calm; neither precipitous nor sluggish. On the flood, it boldly asserts its independence, though sometimes, by way of showing its strength and general forbearance, you may see a hay-stack, or a stray sheep, floating on the unstoppable current. But in general, it winds through a narrow but sweet pastoral valley, with becoming moderation, and even modesty.

Yet peaceful and beautiful as it is, for ages it was the scene of rapine, blood, and battle for all those Border feuds which concentrated on this point. The waters of the Liddel ran red, its green banks dyed with the blood of vassal and lord, Scotchman and Englishman, of Douglas, Hume, Howard, Graham, and Percy. These bold and stirring times formed characters which remained long after reiving had ceased. Elliots, Armstrongs, Jardines, and Johnstones, all left their descendants a spirit of fearless independence and wassail hospitality which remains to this hour. At the time of this story they were still in full vigour; and the incidents of the story illustrate such characters.

The property of Whithaugh has been in the family of the present venerable and kind-hearted proprietors for at least four centuries. Its produce has always provided all the necessaries, and even some of the luxuries of life. Surprisingly, no miser or spendthrift has changed its extent since the days of James V of Scotland. The rental income being free and unencumbered, the owner is just as rich as he wishes to be, able to afford that immemorial hospitality for which the Elliots of Whithaugh continue to be quite celebrated.

A few years ago I heard this tale from old Elliot himself, in the presence of Reverend Mr Barton, worthy minister of Castleton, who can vouch for the truth of what follows...

During the reign of the detestable Charles II, Sir James Johnstone of Westerhall was a well-known persecutor of Covenanters. His mansion was at no great distance from Liddesdale, and he treated himself occasionally to what he termed a Border Chase. Which is to say, he rode with a troop of dragoons along the dale, levying heavy fines and occasionally shooting any stray son of the Covenant caught fleeing to a cave or the morass. In one of these excursions Johnstone encountered the Laird of Whithaugh's poor, imbecile brother, Archy Elliot, who had escaped into the mountains from the man who protected and cared for him. The inoffensive, but perfectly fatuous Archy was known in the neighbourhood by the nickname of "Ah-But-Archy," from his commencing every sentence with the words "Ah-But." He had wandered into a mountain dell; and, unable to extricate himself, at last sat down upon a rock, beneath a tree.

Johnstone and his party were searching for Gilbert Watson, because Gilbert had had his child baptised by the recently ousted minister of the parish. As a result of an 'information' lodged against him by the curate of Applegirth Gilbert was compelled to hide, supposedly in what was called "Fox Den," on the water of Tarras. Johnstone saw the figure of a man seated in the dell, and immediately dismounted from his horse and descended into the hollow with two dragoons.

"Hollo!" shouted Johnstone, in a loud and harsh tone of voice, "Hollo! brother brush-the-heather, what have we here? A Bible, no doubt, and a psalm-tune, and a Covenanting dirge, made up of profanity and high treason in equal proportions. Stir your stumps, old Gibby! Ye're wanted, man, by the guidwife. She can get nae rest without you; and the vile, roaring babby which ye sae lately made a Christian of, took a taste o' the colder air this morn at the top o' Sergeant Pagan's sword. Look, man! Glour, man! You, Gibby! There's the blood o' the yelping brat on the sword yet. Pat Pagan tells me it won't come off; so we'll e'en see if the Tarras water winna wash it oot." Pulling the sword out of the hands of the grim sergeant, he swung it backwards and forwards in the adjoining pool.

In the meantime, Daft Archy had sprung to his feet, and was staring wildly at the company that surrounded him.

"Ah-But, man, ah-but, man, I'm Archy ye ken. Archy Elliot ye ken, ah-but, no kill Archy, ah-but, ah-but, ah-but!"

"None of your Whiggery slang here, ye manting, shamming fool! D'ye think we dinna see that all this foolery is put on, man? D'ye think we dinna ken Gibby Watson o' the Goosedub? Men, do your duty, and secure the traitor!"

The dragoons were starting in to execute their orders, when one of them interfered, and assured his Honour that he was mistaken in the person - for this was the 'daft brither o' the Laird o' Whithaugh.'

"Elliot o' Whithaugh!" exclaimed Johnstone, "Old, canting, traitor-hiding Elliot! I've a good mind to set his house afire about his lugs, and toss this lump of idiocy into the fire, just to feed the flame. Tie the creature to a tree, and we'll go to Elliot's of Whithaugh. It's a thousand to one that 'Gibby God-be-thanked' is snugly lodged in the laird's pantry; or, maybe hiding in the heart o' a peat-stack."

Ignoring the screams and struggles of the innocent Archy, away the party scampered, as if on a holiday excursion, towards the old house of Whithaugh. It had rained hard overnight, and the Liddel was running dark, smooth, and foam-belled. Instead of going about a mile round by the old stone bridge, the whole party fearlessly dashed into the swollen stream, and pushed forward. The opposite bank being steep, as Sergeant Pagan's horse tried to climb out, it fell back into the boiling water with its rider beneath. At once rider and horse were tumbled over and over, and lodged in a deep pool under a steep cliff some yards lower down. Horse and man seemed entangled until, at last, the horse escaped, and made for the further shore. Alas Pagan was never again seen alive. His body was found afterwards some miles lower down the river.

When he found that one of the most tried and trustworthy of his troop, or in other words, one of the most cruel and daring, had paid the forfeit of his own temerity, Johnstone uttered a curse or two in reference to the departed's soul, and swore that he would make old Whithaugh suffer for this. Accordingly, the band trotted towards the front door. But when he demanded entrance, he was told from a window that none would be permitted.

The party had been seen approaching, and their purpose guessed at; and Whithaugh had resolved to defend Gilbert Watson and his premises by force and the assistance of two stout sons, an only daughter of singular beauty, and nearly half-a-dozen ploughmen. This altered the aspect of things somewhat. Johnstone bestowed his usual allowance of curses upon the old man, the house, and all its inmates, then drew from his pocket what he termed a "Lauderdale," or high commission, which entitled him to search out, sack, and if necessary, put to the sword all manner of traitors and conventiclers. Having read it, he was proceeding to open the front door by force, when poor Archy was heard fast approaching under the conduct of his keeper.

"Ah-but, ah-but," said Archy "ah-but, no kill, no kill, ah-but, tie, ah-but, tie, tree! tree! tree!" pointing to the trees which surrounded the green.

"Give the old cutter a broadside," said Johnstone, retreating from the door to give freedom to the men; and immediately the whole front windows were lying in shining fragments inside and outside the apartments. Luckily, seeing the preparation being made, everybody had stood aside from the windows, and no one was injured. Archy's keeper was attempting to keep him out of harm's way, but, by a sudden effort, Archy escaped, and rushed upon the assailants armed with a pitchfork he found in the stack-yard, lodging the weapon in the flanks of a trooper's horse before his rider could turn him round. This so incensed the soldier, that he instantly pulled out his holster pistol, and shot the poor half-witted lad through the head. Repeating his well-known exclamation, "ah-but, ah-but" as he fell, Archie died in an instant.

Seeing how matters were going on outside, old Whithaugh, who had so far acted merely on the defensive, discharged a fowling-piece at the captain of the band. The ball grazed his bridle hand, and blood flowed from the slight injury. This so incensed the leader that he immediately ordered the stackyard and out-houses to be set on fire, vowing that if the traitor were not given up, he would burn down the Ha' house likewise, and leave nothing unburned about the steading. Already the cattle had begun to roar at the stake, and the hens and turkeys to escape from the flaming stackyard, when out Whithaugh issued, surrounded by his resolute supporters, armed with grapes, pitchforks, and other lethal weapons.

Seeing how things were, Gilbert himself sprang out of the hay-stack he had been hidden in, which was now starting on fire. Throwing himself between the combatants, he called aloud for an armistice, and offered to surrender. Then the beautiful Helen Elliot rushed out between them, and fell onto her knees, praying that her father's grey hairs might be spared. This altered matters considerably. The cattle were saved, and some of the flames were extinguished.

Having gained his object, though at the expense of life and much valuable property, Johnstone gave orders for a retreat. Gilbert Watson was placed upon a dragoon's saddle, in a very inconvenient position, whilst the rider sat comfortably behind him. Johnstone bestowed some extravagant, but unwelcome praises upon the personal charms of fair Helen, then the whole party, except the wounded horse, and the man who had drowned, marched up the dale, deciding that they would not risk their lives in the swollen flood.

At the bridge stands a little public-house, about half a mile from the manse of Castleton. Into this public-house the party betook themselves to refresh, whilst the curate of Castleton was sent for. He had often informed Johnstone about the poor people in hiding, who had fled to the mountains, glens, moss and caves, for their lives' and consciences' sake. This curate had a little bandy-legged body, with a large aquiline nose, a hunched back, and a most sinister squint. His church was deserted apart from the family in the small change-house, and one or two farmers who were in fear of suspicion and consequent spoliation, so they were in the habit of occasionally attending. Like his neighbours of the curacy, he had been imported, ready made, from Aberdeen, with all its strange dialect, and all its stranger leanings to oppression and Episcopacy.

The manse was then situated high up the hill, on the brink of a precipice. When Johnstone's messenger arrived the curate was with a person, being given the important information that a conventicle was to gather this very evening at at Dead-Water, a large mountain-moss situated on the Border, and source of the river Tyne on the one side, and the Liddel on the other. The curate hot-footed it to the Brig change-house with this intelligence, accompanied by Johnstone's messenger. A few minutes after talking to Johnstone the men were given their marching orders.

The prisoner Gilbert Watson was locked in a small thatched byre attached to the gavel of the dwelling-house, under the guard of a dragoon. Several attempts were made by his friends to get the soldier withdrawn but they proved ineffectual. Meanwhile, the night began to darken, with soft-falling snow, which made the ground all white around. Gilbert had said his prayers, sung the 121st Psalm, and was preparing to rest himself, with a cow and her calf as his companions, when he thought he heard a voice whispering to him from the roof of the byre.

It was indeed a voice, and a friendly one too for it said, "Here! Here!" A staff was thrust through a small aperture in the thatch. Gilbert moved towards the place, and in whispers exceedingly low, heard that an opening in the roof was to be made for his escape. Meantime, Gilbert kept constantly moving about so that the watch at the door might think he was still in his keeping. When a hole large enough had been made, Gilbert was pulled up by the arms and shoulders, and carried through the snow and down the glen on the back of a strong man, with amazing speed.

The soldier had heard the noise, and immediately hailed his prisoner. When there was no answer he entered, and discovered the escape. Immediately he ran round the byre, but in doing so, he felt his feet entangled in a rope, and when he put down his hands, he was caught by the waist in a strong fox-trap. This made him roar aloud for help; but before the innkeeper could give him any assistance, the prisoner had considerable time to escape.

In fact, with noiseless speed, the strong man had borne Gilbert a considerable distance. Then, setting him down in the snow, he untied his shoes, and putting them heels foremost, and thus reversed, fastened them by strings to his feet. "Now," said the man, as he parted, "now for Castle Hermitage and its dungeon! Till to-morrow morning, when assistance will be rendered!"

So saying, the man left, and disappeared in the snow amongst the woods. Gilbert did as he was instructed, and in about an hour reached the dismal solitude of Castle Hermitage. There this persecuted man remained till the following morning, on the very same straw remaining from when poor Sir Alexander Ramsay of Dalhousie was starved to death by Sir William Douglas.

Meantime, Johnstone had discovered that he was sent on a fool's errand, as there was no such meeting as the curate had told him of was about to take place at the Dead-Water-Moss. He returned in no very good humour. First to the manse of Castleton, where he proposed throwing the curate over the precipice underneath his window, and then to the inn at the Brig-end of Liddel Water about midnight. By now his rage was converted into fury at the trick which he knew had been played upon him. He stamped, swore, and blasphemed all through the night, drinking and eating mutton ham by turns, and swearing to his men that at dawn, they would give chase to the old fox.

As day broke, so chase was given, hither and thither. As the snow had been undisturbed from the time of the escape till morning, it was naturally guessed that the footsteps of the pursued might still be traced. Johnstone, with a few of his men, set out in the track from the back of the byre, and made certain work of it till they came to the bottom of the glen where the footsteps were confused, and then seemed to have made off towards Whithaugh. Having despatched a strong body to follow the footsteps, Johnstone and his men set to tracing the steps back to whence they came, and rode over the rising ground, coming down at once on the old towers of Castle Hermitage.

Here the truth appeared to be obvious. There were two tracks, one approaching and one departing, and they immediately inferred that the one they tracked had first arrived at the castle keep, but had then gone on to the glen. In fact, the strong man of last evening had arrived earlier, with provisions and refreshment to the dungeon, but the footprints left earlier by Gilbert looked as if he had departed. Johnstone very naturally took the two sets of foot-prints to be one person, for one was advancing and the other retreating.

Off they set at full gallop whilst Gilbert and one of Whithaugh's ploughmen made the best of their way in the opposite direction, and ultimately separated within sight of Hawick. The honest ploughman, well satisfied with his dexterity, returned to the broad and fertile acres of Whithaugh; whilst Gilbert Watson ultimately reached some friends who lived in the Cowgate of Edinburgh, and by that means he escaped entirely.

The shoes which contributed so greatly to the escape of Gilbert Watson were presented as a memorial to the Elliot family, and are still shown to the curious by the present worthy proprietor of Whithaugh. After this unfortunate 'raid,' Johnstone became morose and peevish, more than usual. He seemed to suffer great mental agony and one morning was found dead in his bed. Helen Elliot, the fair maid of Whithaugh, was wooed and won by a Charteris of Empsfield; and the present honourable family of that title are descended from her.

So ends my tale of shoes 'Hysteron Proteron' or, 'the Shoes Reversed.'

Retold by Andrea Williams

The Shoes Reversed companion piece

The Shoes Reversed, written by Professor Thomas Gillespie, appears in Wilson's Tales, Volume 20, within 'Gleanings of the Covenant'. It is set in 'The Killing Time(s)' of Scotland. As explained in background pieces in Wilson's Tales of the Borders, Revival Edition Volume 4, religious beliefs of royalty, and their imposition on the Scottish people, resulted in another vicious period of history. This followed the turbulent reiving times, vividly captured in Border Ballads. Branding, burning, raping, pillaging and murder had become commonplace across southern Scotland from the 13th century. Violent acquisitions of land, property and stock, were followed by 'hot trods' doing their savage best to retrieve the same.

The Tale reports on the strong and independent characteristics developed by reiving clans, remaining "long after reiving ceased", and being "still in full vigour" when life was disrupted by religious differences and non-conformists began to be killed without trial. In general, border clans aligned themselves with the oppressed, feeling embittered themselves by James's earlier 'pacification of the borders'.

The non-conformists became known as Covenanters, referring to the covenants by which they maintained Presbyterianism as the only Scottish religion. They did not espouse royalty and its ornate religious practices. They refused to align with Charles II's uncompromising Presbyterianism, heavy with episcopacy, that is government of the church by bishops. Hated by so many, he would surely have been considered the "detestable Charles 11" of the Tale. There was an escalation of conventicles. These were secret services of worship suiting Covenanters' simpler preferences. Informants frequently used local intelligence to identify and share locations, allowing persecutions of a gruesome nature. Individuals and whole families took to the hills, hiding in caves and remote locations.

'The Killing Time' is described by some authorities as being specific to 1684-85. Other sources give different dates and add plurality to the 'Time.' The specified years may have seen the worst of persecutions but before, and afterwards, many Covenanters continued in fear of their lives. John Howie in Scots Worthies identified a much lengthier period of persecution, during which he estimated 18,000 people were pursued and severely mistreated, with significant numbers murdered in cold blood by the King's Troops and their supporters. Eradication of dissenters, it was hoped, would remind everyone of royalty's divine right to rule, or, in the view of those being pursued, "the right divine of kings to govern wrong". (as stated in another Wilson's Tale: The Covenanter's Bridal, in Volume 2 of the Mackenzie edition of 1900).

The levels of persecution described in The Shoes Reversed confirms that perpetrators had no limits. Sir James Johnstone, as a King's Man in pursuit of Gilbert Watson, claimed to have law on his side. Johnstones have lived at Westerhall House in Dumfriesshire for centuries and a "Border chase" into Liddesdale would have been achievable. For added interest, a Johnstone of Westerhall is remembered for gentler actions. Sir William Pulteney (nee Johnstone) married an heiress, took her surname in 1767, and so became Britain's wealthiest man, and renowned patron of Thomas Telford and Robert Adam.

Returning to the curate who provided an "information" prompting Johnstone's pursuit of Gilbert Watson, his "Applegirth" is now known as Applegarth Town, close to the River Annan and Lockerbie.

Gilbert Watson, the non-conformist who was being pursued, is referred to as "of the Goosedub", i.e. of the goose pond. Goosedub Moor is near Dumfries and his origins, we assume, lay in that direction.

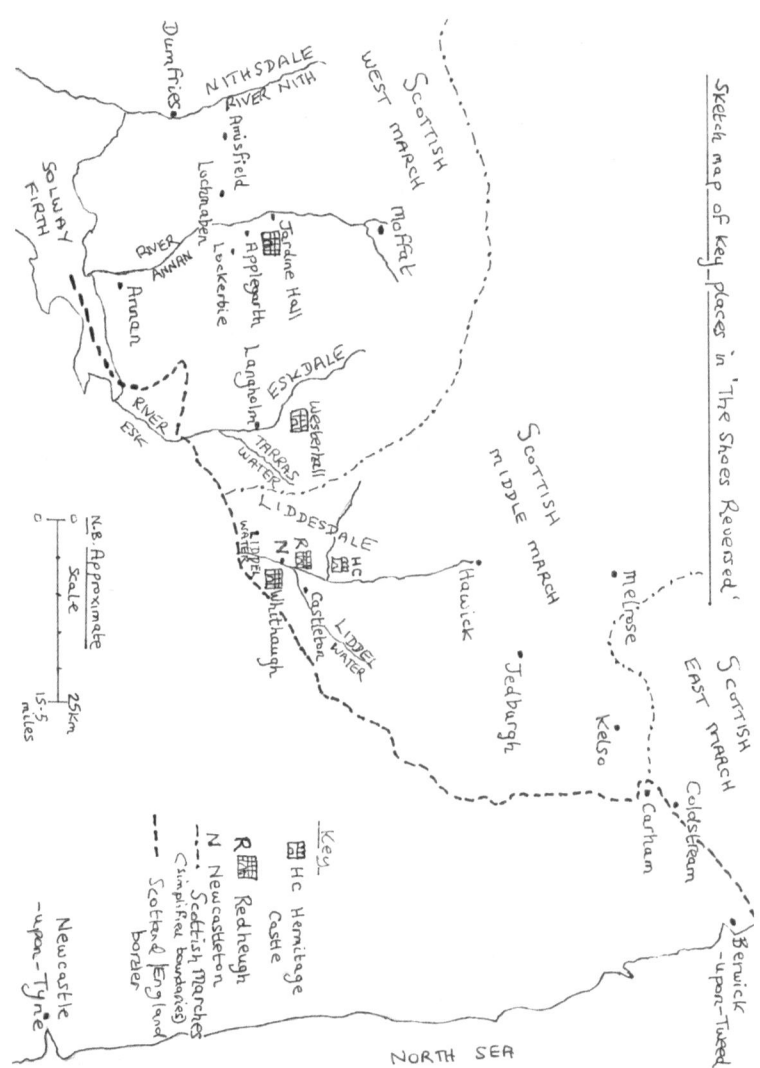

With this background established, there is much to explore concerning other components of the Tale. Clan and place names confirm the setting in the south of the Scottish Middle March and the east of the Scottish West March (designations of the 16th and 17th centuries). In 21st century terms, this comprises the south-eastern area of the Scottish Borders, south of Hawick and east of Langholm, still known as Liddesdale, and the western area of Dumfries and Galloway around Lockerbie/Lochmaben (see map).

The named clans and clan lines, with horrific reiving histories, have long lived here. The man credited as provender of the tale within The Shoes Reversed is "Old Elliot" of Whithaugh, which, the Tale claims, has been an Elliot residence "for at least four centuries". Whithaugh still exists, visible in winter through bare-branched trees across the Liddel Water near Newcastleton. Originally built by Armstrongs, an 'Elliot of Whithaugh' gravestone in Castleton Cemetery suggests that members of Clan Elliot acquired it before 1667. A photograph of a Mary Slee watercolour, representing Whithaugh Tower in 1780,(according to accompanying text), has been kindly shared by Margaret Eliott, Clan Chief. The National Record of the Historic Environment states that the tower was destroyed around 1770 with only foundations left in 1795.

During the 'action' at Whithaugh, the stack-yard is mentioned. This would be within the barmkin, a walled protection for stock and crops. James V's 1535 Act of Parliament ordered erection of barmkins around clan residences for added security. If "expedient", according to the Act, towers could also be built. Johnstone refers, in the Tale, to Whithaugh's "Ha' house" (Hall House). These were first built in the 13th century as two-storey rectangular buildings with ground floor storage and living

The Gravestone of Elliot of Whithaugh

quarters above. By 1300, greater protection was needed and towers were often added. Less than a century later, James VIth of Scotland and 1st of England undertook his 'pacification of the borders', destroying the majority of towers. The tower of Whithaugh did well to survive. It appears from the painting to have been rebuilt as a fortified dwelling incorporating a tower, rather than retained as an original Ha' house. In the Tale, "Old Elliot" was well- sheltered in Whithaugh, with others, defending his family and Gilbert Watson. These thick-walled properties gave great protection from the 14th to the 17th century. The last Elliot descendant sold Whithaugh in 1924. Whithaugh Elliot hospitality is thus, sadly, no more, but thrives at Redheugh, Clan Seat of the Eliotts, (a few miles from Whithaugh), where Eliotts have lived almost continuously for nearly 500 years.

The varied spellings of the surname ("Elliot" featuring throughout the Tale) are detailed in the Clan's comprehensive history. The Elliots: The Story of a Border Clan was written by The Dowager Lady Eliott of Stobs and Sir Arthur Eliott, 11th Baronet of Stobs. (grandmother and father of the current Clan Chief). Only the Stobs line have the 'Eliott' spelling. The Whithaugh Elliots are of the same line. When sons of Redheugh and Whithaugh became lawyers, confusion between legal signatories needed to be minimised and the difference was agreed. This may amaze readers who have tried to interpret ancient ink-written documents, when an extra 'i', 't', or 'l' can easily be overlooked.

Clan Eliott genealogy, particularly of the Stobs line, shows Archibald as a frequent Christian name. Perhaps an Archy Elliot of Whithaugh suffered an unfortunate stammer and other challenges. Sadly, even today, the disadvantaged are often ridiculed. In those harrowing times, the torment and isolation of such individuals would have been extreme. The sad reality is that storytellers probably included a disadvantaged character to add 'colour' to their stories.

Returning to Elliot genealogy, the name of Helen does appear. Archy's niece in the Tale, Helen Elliot, was "of singular beauty" and a "fair maid". Such literary descriptors have been frequently used for ladies of Liddesdale. Helen utilised her attributes to calm Johnstone and preserve her father. She later married "a Charteris of Empsfield". The Charteris Clan Seat in East Lothian, was, in the 17th century, in Nithsdale in Dumfriesshire at Amisfield, not Empsfield, presumably an error of transcription in the creation of the story.

To add further clarity regarding place names, the reference to the Minister of Castleton could confuse. Professor Gillespie (1777-1844), would have been aware of the 1790s' clearance of Castleton, remotely situated above Liddesdale, and where, importantly, the cemetery remains today. His Minister was most likely actually 'of Castleton parish' as this parish name continued long after Castleton village was replaced by Newcastleton. A Reverend Barton is recorded as minister of Castleton parish in the 19th century and perhaps enjoyed tales from "old Elliot".

"Castle-Hermitage", to which Gilbert escaped, is now referred to as Hermitage Castle and even in the 17th century this nomenclature appears on maps. In both the original and the re-telling, the reversed word order for the castle's name, was perhaps used by the original author of the Tale to mirror the 'hysteron proteron' of the Tale's title, 'The Shoes Reversed'. This literary and rhetorical device is usually used to emphasise a later action ahead of an earlier one, eg "to put on shoes and socks" - not advised! At the risk of getting pedantic, it would be more accurate to describe the reversal of the words, in both examples, as an example of a "hyperbaton", that is a deliberate departure from the usual word order.

Remotely situated, north west of Newcastleton and with a gruesome past, ghostly tales abound. Sir Arthur Elliot wrote "no-one but the descendant of a Border reiver has dared spend the night within". Marshy surrounds always served its best defence. Their

Castle-Hermitage

cover of thick snow was crucial to Gilbert's survival, coupled with the acumen of his protector, the "strong man", revealed as a Whithaugh ploughman. Without snow to preserve those double, and opposing, footprints, we may have been reading about another Covenanter murder.

As for those significant shoes, thoughtful preservation for posterity seems unlikely. Gilbert would have needed them, worn the right way round, for his journey to Edinburgh and beyond, after which they presumably rotted in distant parts, long after the end of this Tale.

Background by Ros Anderson

New Tales from Berwick's young people

The success of Wilson's Tales meant that new Tales were published to meet popular demand long after Wilson's untimely death.

Aspiring authors from around Scotland submitted tales for consideration and over 20 authors subsequently had Tales published. With that in mind, we have been delighted to join with Berwick Rotary and the Berwick Literary Festival in inviting new Tales to form part of the Revival Edition. For a third year we have done this through an open writing competition in local schools – which this year attracted a record number of entries.

This year's three winners embrace peril at sea, a magical gift and bloody hand-to-hand (or tentacle) combat – all popular themes in the original Tales. We congratulate them all – particularly Becki Richardson, making her second appearance in these pages – and look forward to hearing more of them in years to come!

Joe Lang

River Tweed Adventure Story

Young Writers Competition winner

Chapter 1: The adventure begins

Have you ever been on an adventure?

Last week Johnny and I went on an adventure at the River Tweed. We walked excitedly along the Dock Road and saw the enormous ancient town walls and the incredible huge New Bridge. It was amazing.

After a while, it was getting dark. Then we made it to the river. We built our tent and made a hot, red, warm fire. We had dinner: cream marshmallows and crispy sausages. It was amazing, delicious and yummy. It was midnight. We went into our sleeping bags and went fast asleep – it was amazing.

At dawn I woke up and went fishing for a few hours. When we finished we had 27 fish and cooked them for our breakfast. It was so yummy, and we cooked more than we could eat.

Chapter 2: The adventure

After breakfast we went on a posh speedboat. We were looking for shiny dolphins. We saw five dolphins with smooth skin and they had dash tails and they did backflips.

As if by magic they disappeared at the speed of light. Then a shark as big as a house appeared. It charged at us, looking very hungry. Then it said: "Get out of here or I will eat you!"

The shark had deadly sharp teeth. It looked like a dolphin who had been beaten up. Its fin was smooth and sharp and it was huge with dark navy blue skin.

"Let's get out of here!" said Johnny. We were scared like mad so we blasted the engine and ZOOOM! – away we went back to our camp. Then it was getting dark so we had dinner. We had lovely chicken and sausages. Then we went to bed.

Chapter 3: The escape

The next day we went for a stroll on the baby blue boat. Then a massive octopus came charging at us, spreading its long enormous tentacles. It said: "I will eat you!"

Its large body came out of the water. It was so scary. Me and Johnny were shivering like jelly. It had eight eyes and stared at us. It had smooth skin and bumpy tentacles.

Then we went faster than ever back to camp and packed up and went home.

Our mums said: "Did you have a good camp? Where did you get that shark's tooth from?"

By Youn Zhen, Spittal Community First School

Adventures Around the River Tweed

Young Writers Competition winner

Sylvie yawned. She would be glad when the holidays were over. She was sitting on her bed and staring out of the window at the shimmering river below. The River Tweed glittered and a silver seal frolicked in the moonlight. She closed her eyes and went to sleep.

One hour later, Sylvie woke with a start. She'd been dreaming about an alchemist, Alchemia, who'd promised to show her how to make a stone which was extremely magical. She had to sleep because the enchantment could only be begun at exactly 11:57pm and she'd be tired if she didn't sleep. Alchemia had set an alarm, and that was what had woken her up.

Sylvia sat up. She was no longer on her bed at home, but on a daybed in Alchemia's guest room!

Alchemia was a legendary alchemist who had lived 50 years before Sylvie. Why was she there?

Sylvie got out of bed and went to the wardrobe. She opened it and looked inside, and before her eyes there was a wide range of dresses from a raspberry pink bridesmaid's dress to a blue silken gown.

When she was dressed, Sylvie found a tinkling bell. When she rang it, a voice from the door answered: "Sylvie! It is almost time. Come through, my dear child!"

Sylvie opened the door to reveal a woman with long black hair. She was wearing an intricately embroidered gown, which was the same colour as the daybed Sylvie had been sleeping on. Alchemia took her through to a cluttered office with French doors opening onto a balcony.

Sylvia gasped. The house they were in was underwater! Emerald-green water swirled around them and weeds waved spookily in the semi-darkness. It was an extraordinary sight.

Alchemia took Sylvia to the door of the balcony and picked up a bottle. She divided the contents between two glasses and downed one. She passed the other to Sylvie: "Drink!"

When Sylvie drank the liquid, a strange feeling went down her spine. It was as if an egg had been cracked on the top of her head. Suddenly, Sylvie gasped for air. She couldn't breathe! What was going on? It looked as if Alchemia was experiencing the same feelings: she looked less composed than usual and had gone pink.

Quickly, Alchemia opened the doors and dived through them. She beckoned to Sylvie. With all of her remaining strength, Sylvie launched herself into the water (which was blocked from the office by a force) and landed on the balcony beside Alchemia.

The water surrounding Sylvie felt like a cool breeze. She was breathing like she had gills and didn't need to blink. On the balcony was a large cauldron. It was completely empty – even of water – with another water barrier.

"It is time," announced Alchemia. "Pass me that green bottle."

"This one?"

"No, that one."

"What else do you need?"

"Can you pass me the spoon?"

"Here you go."

"Thanks. Count while I stir."

"One, two, three, four."

"Good. So I added newt blood and stirred…"

"Four times!"

"Yes. Four times, anticlockwise. I know the recipe off by heart, so I can repeat it to you."

"Yes please!"

"Add two drops of newt blood and stir four times. Pound an elderberry to a fine powder. Add it in and stir thrice, clockwise. In another cup, add two parts daffodil essence, one part oak sap and two parts rose petal and sunflower oil. For five minutes, stir it. After every 12 stirs clockwise, stir once anticlockwise. Leave to boil while you mix freshly salted water with powdered bison horn. Your potion should turn lilac. Once you have added your water, it will turn maroon. Put your barrier back and drain your potion of all the water. You should be left with a dark brown syrup which should go into an airtight container in a warm cupboard for 12 hours while it sets into stone."

They were now standing back in Alchemia's untidy office, beside a cupboard which Sylvie closed. She was exhausted. It was 12:27 and Sylvie had been concentrating hard that night, so as to remember everything.

Suddenly, Sylvie remembered Jasmine and Misti, who wouldn't know where she was! Then, Alchemia spoke:

"We will now turn in for the night. I am sure you are exhausted."

"Well, yes…" said Sylvia, vacantly.

"Something is bothering you," said Alchemia curiously. "Pray, tell me your worry."

"Well… I absolutely love it here – it's just… Well, I kind of miss my family and my friends. It will be my birthday soon and, well…"

"I see! But… dear child! Didn't I say? This stone – it's yours! Anyway, do you not live by the River Tweed?"

"Well, yes, but… I don't see what that has to do with anything!"

"Go to bed, child. I'll explain in the morning. You won't understand tonight. You will go back home soon."

Sylvie woke up to Alchemia's voice. "Sylvie! Get up, child. After all, it must be you who removes it, so its allegiance is to you!"

"What?" said Sylvie, blearily.

When Sylvie had woken up, she followed Alchemia to the cupboard where the stone was. At 27 minutes past midday by Alchemia's clock, Sylvie lifted the lid from the container in which Alchemia had placed the stone.

"This," began Alchemia, "is a lapis. It is very rare."

"Um, Al... Alchemia...?" asked Sylvie, "When will I go home?"

"I see you won't be diverted," sighed Alchemia. "I will explain."

"When you went to sleep at your home, you had this stone in your pocket. You had found it on your window sill, and didn't know why it was there. You put it in your pocket and went downstairs for lunch. During lunch, you were talking about me, the alchemist from the past. That evening, you dreamed about me – and because there is a hole in your pocket, the stone was touching you and transported you to the place you were thinking of. The stone can not only transport you to any place in the world but also any moment. This means that it took you from your present to your past. It also took you from your cottage to my house in the river. When you go back to your present, you MUST first go to the morning of the day you dreamed and place the lapis on your window sill before returning to the night of the dream. If you don't place it on the window sill, this won't have happened."

Alchemia stopped. Sylvie said: "So... this wouldn't have happened if this hadn't happened? What...?"

"Time is a loop," continued Alchemia. "Nothing would have happened if nothing had happened, and that is my main study in philosophy. This concept is hard to comprehend. Now, my dear child, it is time for you to go home and replace the stone. All you have to do is hold onto it and think of the morning of the dream and you will go. Follow my instructions, then think of the evening of the dream and you will go back home."

Sylvie looked at Alchemia. She liked her, but she wanted to go back to her family – and friends.

"Don't worry," said Alchemia. "Follow."

Alchemia took Sylvie back to the guest room. She pointed at the wardrobe. "This is for you," she said.

Sylvie gaped. She wasn't sure if Alchemia was joking. It seemed unbelievable, but Alchemia was really generous. "What... do you mean?" Sylvie gasped.

Alchemia smiled. She loved how Sylvie was so modest. It was as if she wasn't used to people being kind to her. "You can have it," said Alchemia.

"Really?" asked Sylvie. "I don't believe it!"

"Really," said Alchemia. "I have no use for it."

"I can have the wardrobe?!" enquired Sylvie.

"And its contents," said Alchemia. Sylvie beamed. She was ecstatic to have new clothes as well as her dress for special occasions, jeans and a t-shirt and her boring school uniform.

"Hold onto the wardrobe and you'll be able to bring it back to your own time and then you will have some more clothes," said Alchemia. "Make sure you tell your parents that you got them from a friend. If they don't accept them I'll throw them down the drain. Now I must say goodbye. Remember my instructions. And by the way – can you visit me once in a while?"

"Yes," said Sylvie. "Should I go?"

Alchemia replied: "Yes."

"Well… see you," said Sylvie. "Goodbye!"

Sylvie closed her eyes and thought about the morning before she'd had the dream. Suddenly, she was spinning through a whirl of colours. They were making her feel dizzy and sick.

Sylvie landed and wobbled slightly. She could hear her past self thundering down the stairs.

She looked around. She was standing facing the window sill. She walked towards it and placed the stone onto it. Then she thought hard about that evening.

Sylvie landed sitting this time. She was exhausted. She lay back and went to sleep.

By Isabel Gilchrist, Tweedmouth Middle School

The End of Land

Young Writers Competition winner

There was a darkness on the beach. Not just in the sky, but a different sort of darkness. A darknes that crept under one's skin and tangled its roots in one's mind; a darkness that fed on the goose bumps of the frightened.

The darkness was slithering through the sand below Beau's feet, lingering in the cool breeze and crawling through the dunes' long grass that seemed never to stop its rhythmic swaying. Beau could smell it in the air; see it in the eyes of his team as they stared apprehensively at the starry sky; feel it in his bones.

It would be a long night for the team. They would count the stars and, once they were done, they would count them again. They would keep counting until it happened.

The sand stretched away in front of Beau and then disappeared below the gentle waves that seemed to glisten in the light of the moon. By the sea, Beau could see Julian, his hands deep in his pockets as he gazed at the water kissing his shoes. He, too, seemed to glow in the moonlight, like Beau's own star. Tonight, he would rely on Julian like the Three Wise Men relied on the Star of Bethlehem.

Beau made his way towards the sand's edge, standing next to Julian. When Julian continued to stare at the sea, Beau nudged him with his shoulder.

"Hey," he said. "Something interesting down there?"

Julian didn't look up, but Beau saw his chest rise and fall as he sighed. "It's odd, don't you think,"

Julian said at last, "that we're stood on the very edge of land? A few meters further and we'd no longer be in England. We'd be alone."

"I suppose," Beau replied, watching Julian's eyes dart across the shallow waves below them. "But you could say the same thing in Berwick, not just of the sea but of the Scottish border, too. That's just how life is, living in the Borders."

Julian's brow furrowed. "But we live on a different border, don't we? The border between life and death. So do the rest of the team." As he spoke, he glanced behind them, up at the tall dunes that hid their co-workers. "We could die tonight."

"We could die at any point."

"But the chances increase when you're fighting aliens."

Julian had spoken louder than expected, and Beau flinched. He wanted to comfort his friend, but he knew Julian was right. That was the source of the darkness looming over them, after all: the knowledge that tonight they would put their lives on the line to save the people of the Borders. They would sacrifice their safety and take on the ship due to land on Cocklawburn beach.

Of course, they'd had training and they had been mentally preparing since it was first announced at Berwick Town Hall that volunteers were needed for battle, after the UFO had been spotted and NASA had deemed it 'extremely dangerous'. Beau had bravely stepped forward, and had kept his brave demeanour since. Now, however, he could feel it slipping.

"You're right," Beau said, taking Julian's hand, "but we can do this."

Julian looked to Beau, and Beau could see the fear in his eyes, warring with months of hard work and years of innocence. He was terrified, but he smiled at Beau nonetheless.

"Yeah," he said, "we ca-"

Julian didn't finish his sentence, as the two of them were catapulted backwards into the sand. Beau sat up, watching as the stars disappeared behind a gargantuan thing in the sky. It looked like a giant squid, with tentacles that waved in the air, slowing as it neared land. The sand was whipping through the air and the sea was shrinking back as the ship descended.

Beau dragged his eyes away from the scene, searching for the rest of the team, but they had vanished. It was just him and Julian.

Julian, who was sprinting towards the water.

Beau got to his feet, running after Julian as the ship hovered just above the sea. He held his arm over his face, trying to shield his eyes from the flying sand as he stumbled to the end of land. He almost didn't notice Julian stop suddenly, narrowly avoiding crashing into him on the damp sand. Beau looked up at the ship above them, its long tentacles battering the air. It seemed to be glowing, a long rectangle of light appearing on its stomach. The light was growing, getting longer until –

"It's letting them out!" Julian shouted.

Simultaneously, they reached into their pockets, each pulling out a small, metal box. Beau tapped the box against his hand and a long, blue blade extended from it. He looked to Julian, as Julian released his own sword, the two of them nodding before charging into the water, just as the first alien dropped from the ship.

The alien landed in the sea with an epic splash that momentarily blinded Beau. When he recovered, the creature was in front of him. It was scaly, with huge black eyes and tentacles for limbs. It rose above Beau on its hind legs and lashed out, causing Beau to stumble backwards. He regained his balance and swung his blade, narrowly avoiding the alien as it swerved and lunged towards him, knocking him off his feet.

Beau felt the sting of salt in his eyes as the alien held him underwater. He flailed his arms, the sea pushing against his blade with mighty force. His lungs burned and chest ached, but he continued to fight against the creature's hold until the world began to spin, his vision going black…

The alien released suddenly, collapsing sideways, and then Beau was being dragged from the water.

He gasped, coughing up blood as he sat and looked around him.

Julian was running away from him, soaked from head to toe, heading straight for a group of aliens further down the beach. In fact, they were not just down the beach, they were everywhere. Some sprinting towards the dunes, some following Julian and others coming towards Beau. He clambered to his feet, head still spinning slightly, and pounced into battle.

The aliens passed him in a blur of muddy scales and tentacles as Beau spun gracefully through the air, his blade slicing through each body that came within reach. His sword was an extension of his arm, obeying him and only him as it pierced necks and punctured eyes. Beau could feel the adrenaline rushing through his veins, the air on his sweaty face. He was winning, aliens becoming corpses before his very eyes until –

"Beau!"

Beau turned in the direction from which has name had been called, his eyes landing on Julian, surrounded, his face bloody and sword nowhere to be seen.

Suddenly, Beau no longer cared about the aliens. He sprinted through the sand, his eyes fixed on the aliens closing in on Julian. His legs burned with the effort, his heart pounding in his tired chest, but he didn't stop. He ran like he could do nothing else – like the sky itself would cave in if he dared to slow down. He pushed through sand, leaped over seaweed, stumbled over pebbles. He could see Julian, see the sweat on his face, the blood in his hair. Just a bit further. He was so close.

But the aliens were closer.

Julian's scream seemed to ripple through the air as a tentacle was thrust through his abdomen. The aliens jeered, watching Julian's body hit the sand.

Beau felt the air leave his lungs as he crashed into one of the aliens, his sword slicing its head clean off. He whirled on the others, hacking through body after body, rage the only thing keeping him on his feet. He swung and stabbed and sliced until the group of creatures lay around him, and then he collapsed onto the cold, bloody sand.

The blade fell from Beau's hand as he crawled towards Julian, who lay sprawled just metres away.

Beau's hand trembled as he reached for Julian's, his fingers sliding over Julian's wrist in search of a pulse he knew he wouldn't find.

The world seemed to have slowed down, the enemies behind him silent. They were no longer an issue. The aliens could rip the Borders to shreds for all Beau cared.

He let his hair fall over his face, swallowing back the taste of salt and blood in his mouth. He pried his eyes away from Julian and turned towards the sea, preparing for his own end.

However, the beach was bare. There were no aliens, no ship. There was nothing but a group of blood-spattered people by the water.

The team.

They noticed Beau, and one of them nodded in his direction, silently saying They're gone. It's over.

Beau dropped his head, unable to feel the relief he knew he should. He could think of nothing but who he should have been celebrating with, and who he would never celebrate anything with again.

Julian had been right, Beau thought. They really did live on the border between life and death. And only one of them had stayed on the correct side.

By Becki Richardson, Berwick Academy

The Contributors

ANDREW AYRE, a resident of Tweedmouth, founded the Wilson's Tales Project in 2013 to celebrate and revive interest in Wilson's Tales and some of the local stories and heritage embedded in them.

He first became aware of the Tales as a child, when the title was given to someone to perform as a New Year charade. Now an accountant by profession, he has maintained a keen interest in history, literature and local events. He is currently reading his way through the Tales and researching for future events, publications and talks.

www.wilsonstales.co.uk

SHEILA VICKERS is an inveterate sketcher. She has a fascination for portraits and characters which explains her history of 'On The Spot' portraits and animals at showgrounds and shopping centres.

The prize of a portable paint set on the ITV programme Watercolour Challenge in 2001 unleashed the desire to capture the essence of characters and their lives wherever she could. This passion has caused her style to evolve naturally into being more illustrative. This has neatly dovetailed with her interest in reading historical novels and for the illustrations for this book.

Sheila can be contacted through her website **www.sheilavickersart.com**

DENISE BRADSHAW was born, brought up and educated in Berwick upon Tweed. Lucky enough to have her interest in reading and literature nurtured by Derek Butler when studying English at Berwick High School and has never stopped loving words, stories or language since then. Using the techniques of good story tellers she continue to effectively present case facts and relevant circumstances in her work as a lawyer. Now living in Ipswich and working mainly in the British Indian Ocean she still loves returning home to Berwick to spend time with family, touch base with her roots and regroup.

FORDYCE MAXWELL oldest of a family of nine from Cramond Hill Farm, Cornhill on Tweed, was educated at Berwick Grammar School and Harper Adams Agricultural College. He has been a journalist since 1967. Much of that time was with *The Scotsman* as agricultural and rural affairs editor, columnist, diarist, Parliamentary sketch writer, feature writer, leader writer and book reviewer. He has freelanced for many other newspapers and magazines and continues to do so, including as Halidon in the Tweeddale Press. He has received the MBE for services to journalism and the Scottish Newspaper Editors' award for lifetime achievement.

JOE LANG began his writing career as a journalist, playwright and advertising copywriter. He started a London-based communications consultancy business, which he ran for 30 years before moving to Berwick and rediscovering the joys of freelance life.

joe@kaineslang.com

KEITH RYAN was born on the right side of the Tweed at Castle Hills Maternity Home and educated at Berwick Grammar School. He is a solicitor by trade, historian by nature, and Lisbon Lion in his dreams. Author of Bloody Berwick, a history of the town when it stood centre stage in three centuries of Anglo-Scottish medieval warfare, he has his boots by his bed for when the call comes from Celtic Park.

keithryan3@aol.com   www.bloodyberwick.com

MICHAEL A. FENTY is a retired GP living in Coldingham. He has been writing for many years – initially articles for medical magazines and later, after retirement, drama.

Michael's play *The Resurrection Man* – based on the letters and trial documents of local doctor George Laurie, tried in 1820 for grave robbing – was performed by the New Strides Theatre Company; and in 2013 he contributed four short plays to a dramatised walk in the Lammermuirs – *The Footsteps of Flodden*. In 2016, his play Tibbie Tamson was performed by the Borders Youth Theatre

The Royal Raid and *The Monks of Dryburgh* were the first two dramatisations for Wilson's Tales. His next, *The Monomaniac*, was performed at Paxton House in 2014 and can still be seen on youtube with **www.youtube.com/watch?v=Yps8-uo8RD4&feature=youtu.b**

Michael's blog *Gangril Days* is at **http://gangrildays.blogspot.co.uk/**

NICK JONES recently moved to Northumberland after years milling organic stoneground flour and organising arts projects in Cumbria. He writes short stories and plays, the most recent inspired by Northumbrian culture, history, tourism, watermills, compost heaps, oceanic plastic, and rubbish in general. Currently researching for a book about Edinburgh's Railway Network with grandson Rowan Harris-Jones

nicolasjbjones@gmail.com and www.jonesnick@wordpress.com

MICHAEL OLIVER is a retired lecturer with a strong interest in history subjects. He lives with his wife, two cats and five ducks near Wooler. He is the author of three published nautical novels set in the Napoleonic period. His hobbies include spinning wool and rebuilding old spinning wheels, researching the history of Northumberland railways, writing and gardening.

ROS ANDERSON moved to the Scottish Borders from Derbyshire with her husband and daughter in 2002, to work as an NHS pharmacist. During a varied career she wrote for academic teaching texts and yearned for creative opportunities: a post-retirement creative writing course and participation in the Borders Writers' Forum, Kelso Writers' Group and Melrose Literary Society provided great inspiration. Her contributions feature in two recent Borders Writers' Forum anthologies: Waverley and Other Railways and Abridged.

ANDREA WILLIAMS divides her time among seemingly random interests. Turning timber into sawdust, with firewood and occasional furniture as a by-product. Writing short stories – some science fiction, some short science fiction. Practising old skills such as breadmaking and dry stone walling.

Resurrecting old artefacts such as pit saws and PC-DOS. "Now that I'm able to look back at mid-life crises from the far side," she says, "Most of life falls into its correct perspective – which is to say that today's pace of life is best viewed from the roadside rather than the driver's seat."

JIM HERBERT has lived in Berwick for 40 years and worked in the heritage industry for the past 20. He loves the history of Berwick-upon-Tweed, Northumberland and the Borders. As well as being a historian he is a designer, actor, technician and siege engineer!

Jim runs Berwick Time Lines, a service offering, among other things, regular tours and talks. He writes a regular Berwick Time Lines blog. Dedicated to Berwick's rich history, he researches stories of the town, its people and buildings, often discovering new truths about the past. He also loves prog rock and playing pool.

For more information about services and Jim's blog, visit **www.berwicktimelines.com** and **www.berwicktimelines.tumblr.com**